OPERATION FURY

SUSAN HAYES

ABOUT THE BOOK

She's fighting for survival. He's fighting for her soul.

Nyx was created to be the perfect killer, with death and violence encoded in her DNA. After years of tests, torments, and trials designed to push her to her breaking point, she's survived by focusing on one thing –revenge.

Nova Force investigator Eric Erben lost someone he cared about. Now he's on a mission to fulfill her last request - free her sister from the shadowy group holding her captive. Rescuing Nyx from her captors is the easy part. Saving her from herself will be a battle only love can win.

Copyright © 2020 Susan Hayes

Operation Fury (Book #3 of Nova Force Series)

First E-book Publication

Cover Art: Mina Carter

Published by: Black Scroll Publications Ltd

ISBN: 978-1-988446-59-2

For my Mum and Dad, for supporting me even when they thought I was crazy. And for my best friend, Karen, for putting up with me when I was definitely nuts.
This book is also dedicated to Heidi and Jenn, for their tireless cheerleading, amazing friendship, and general shenanigans.

PROLOGUE

IN A GALAXY FILLED with different species, cultures, and governments, there is only one constant: trade.

In the aftermath of the Resource Wars, the surviving corporations grew strong enough to rival any government, affecting everything from colonization plans to intergalactic law.

To counter their influence and check their powers, the Interstellar Armed Forces created a new division, Nova Force. Their mission – ensure the corporations play by the rules, by any means necessary.

Welcome to Nova Force. The last line of defense between the citizens of the galaxy and the corporations who believe that the laws are flexible, and everything is for sale, for the right price.

CHAPTER ONE

Nyx was shoved through the door into her cell by her silent guards, and she barely made it to the bare cot at the back of her cell before her legs gave out. She collapsed onto the bed, her lips sealed against a groan. She had blocked the pain for now, though it was a temporary reprieve. Not even her cybernetic modifications allowed her to ignore pain forever.

The door slid into place, leaving nothing but a blank wall. There was an almost invisible seam marking the entry, so fine she couldn't fit a hair between it and the hardened steel of the wall. She'd tested the strength of both door and wall more times than she could count, but it had defeated her. It had taken her captors years to manage it, but they'd finally built a cell she couldn't escape.

Not that getting out of her cell accomplished anything except staving off the boredom for a little while. She was being held on a space station far from the standard shipping routes, a fact she'd been able to ascertain from the crew's complaints about the lack of fresh food and other supplies. Her rations consisted of flavorless food tabs and the occasional bowl of synthesized algae broth. It kept her alive, but she had no idea what fresh *anything* was like. Her water and air were recycled, and the jumpsuit she wore had been laundered so often it had lost all traces of shape and color.

She stayed sprawled on the cot until her legs stopped shaking and her hands were steady. The tests always did this to her. She might not feel the pain, but her body still recognized the trauma she endured as they tried to force her mind to accept the programming. Today's trials had included replacing one of the implants at the base of her skull. They needed her awake and aware during the tests so they could assess their progress and any changes. She'd learned early on that if she didn't cooperate, they'd deactivate her ability to block pain. It was a brutal lesson, one she never wanted to experience again. There were other ways to defy her captors.

Nyx got to her feet. If she stayed down much longer, it would look like weakness.

She went to the tiny sink and cleaned up as best she could, using the trickle of tepid water and a washcloth she'd liberated from stores during her last escape. For some reason, they'd let her keep it.

They. Them. After all these years, she still didn't know who held her prisoner. She'd been created by the

Astek Corporation about a year before the war ended, but she'd been separated from her batch siblings once her unique abilities were discovered. Since then, she'd been moved from lab to lab, subjected to a lifetime of tests, trials, and torments. All she had was a name whispered into her mind by one of the strongest of her clones during a moment of telepathic connection. The Gray Men.

There were no mirrors in her cell, so she used her fingers to assess her injuries. Her medi-bots had already sealed the wounds, and she estimated they'd be fully healed in two hours or so. If they fed her, it would happen faster, but she doubted that would happen. It was in their best interest to keep her weak, so they made sure she never got enough food or rest to be at her best.

Despite that, she stayed strong. They hadn't broken her yet, and they never would. She'd die before that happened, and she had no intention of dying until after she'd taken her revenge. In the words of an old Earth poet whose work she'd encountered one of the rare times she'd been allowed books to read: she had promises to keep and miles to go before she could sleep.

ERIC WAS CONVINCED that weddings were a special kind of hell. It was bad enough the members of his team seemed to be falling in love like it had the gravitational force of a black *fraxxing* hole, but to celebrate the fact, he had to don his dress uniform and go make polite conversation with groups of beings—most of whom he had to salute, including the bride and groom.

As happy as he was for his commanding officer, Dax Rossi, and his new wife, Trinity, being at this reception stirred memories he didn't want. The last time he'd been at a wedding, he'd met Echo. She'd been special. Then she'd died, and he'd learned she was an assassin with a long list of targets, some of them his friends.

He shook off his stormy mood, shoved the memories aside, and headed for the bar at the far end of the reception hall. If he was stuck at this party for another few hours, he wasn't doing it sober.

He took in the decorations while he walked, and grudgingly admitted the place looked good. Nova Force's operations base out here on the Drift was small and utilitarian, like everything else on the space station. The drab walls of the largest briefing room had been festooned with red and gold bunting, and light cubes filled the space with cheerful lights that shifted slowly between colors, adding a festive air. Tables were draped with red tablecloths strewn with some kind of glittery golden confetti the janitorial bots would probably be trying to eradicate for weeks. The room wasn't that large, and he had to navigate a crowd of well dressed and exuberant wedding guests to get to the bar. By the time he made it, he was downright parched.

The bartender looked up and grinned at him. "Hey, Magi, one of your usual?"

Eric grunted an affirmative and claimed a seat.

"Make it a double. I didn't expect to see you behind the bar tonight, Kit. I thought you'd be enjoying the party with your wife and brother."

Kit shook his head as he worked. "Not tonight. This is our gift to the newlyweds. Luke and Zura handled the food, and I'm providing the drinks."

"Who is watching the twins?"

"They're with Nan."

"No one is going to mess with those kids with Nan on the job." One of his teammates had gone on an undercover mission and come back with a new life, including a girlfriend and a little boy they were in the process of adopting. Faced with the daunting task of juggling an instant family and a military career, Dante had ended up hiring Nan, a surprisingly spry senior, to help out.

Kit snorted as he set Eric's drink in front of him. "She's something else. I heard she's banned from the male strip clubs across the station. I don't want to know why."

"Me either." He took a sip of his drink. "Did you know Dante caught her teaching Nico how to pick locks the other day? When he raised hell about it, she informed him that she was teaching the boy the practical application of physics."

Kit cocked his head to one side. "She's not wrong about that. Just do me a favor and don't mention that to Royan or Owen. They'll try to corrupt my kids a thousand different ways if they think they can justify it as educational."

7

Eric put his drink down and tapped his fingers. "They won't hear it from me. I'm a professional keeper of secrets."

"More like the professional finder of secrets. Not that I'm complaining. The work you and your team do makes the galaxy a safer place." Kit's normally cheerful expression turned solemn. "You know why our bar is called the Nova Club?"

"No, actually."

"It's not a coincidence. My batch siblings and I were freed without any issues, but we know many weren't. Nova Force were the ones who put their lives on the line to save the cyborgs from the corporations. We named the club for all of you."

Eric let that sink in, a little stunned. "You never said anything before. Do the others know?"

"I've never mentioned it to anyone until now. I just thought you looked like you could use a bit of good news." Kit leaned in. "Memories?"

"Yeah."

Kit's family had been Echo's employers. They'd been wounded by her betrayal too.

"You getting anywhere with your side project?"

Eric took another pull at his drink before answering. It didn't totally wash away the bitter taste of defeat, but it helped. "It's slow going."

"Echo believed in you. If anyone can find this Nyx person, it's you."

"A couple of months ago, I'd have agreed with you." He mustered a grin. "I'm one of the best at what I do, after all, but there's someone out there who's at least as good as I am, and they don't have to play by the rules I do." And that was the *fraxxing* problem. He was bound by galactic law and military protocol.

Kit grunted in commiseration. "It's frustrating, but you'll think of something. It's what you guys do, right?" More guests approached the bar, and Kit stepped away to serve them, leaving Eric alone with his thoughts.

Protecting people from the corporations was what they were supposed to do, but he hadn't done that for Echo. She'd left him one last message, and her words still haunted him.

"I'm sorry, Eric. What we had was never meant to be. I was dead before we ever met. If I meant anything at all to you, save her. You're the only one who can."

Save her. He'd been trying for months, but so far he hadn't been able to find Nyx, never mind mount a rescue. Her name had been in the files Echo had given to his side just before she died, but a name was all he had. That, and a mention of something called the Fury Project, which appeared to be related to the creation of cyborg assassins like Echo.

So far, he hadn't found anything that the higher-ups would accept as actionable intel, and every time he got close to something solid, the trail would fizzle out faster than a shooting star. Someone was playing games with him, and he was running out of moves.

He stared into the dark crimson liquid at the bottom

of his glass. No, that wasn't accurate. He was out of *legal* moves.

He drained the last of his drink and stood, suddenly certain of what his next move would be, and the risks that came with it. He'd joined the IAF to avoid going to prison, and they watched him carefully to make sure he didn't revert back to old habits.

If he was going to do this his way, he'd have to be smart about it. Good thing he was one of the best hackers in the galaxy, or this might be a challenge. He could almost feel his data ports tingling in anticipation. He was going to find this missing cyborg and fulfill a dying woman's last request. He hadn't been able to save Echo, but he *would* save Nyx.

CHAPTER TWO

OLD HABITS really do die hard.

Eric was done playing by the IAF's rules. It was time to get this done – his way.

It had taken him less than an hour to find an abandoned data node on one of the maintenance levels, secure the area, and set up a simple warning system to alert him if anyone came too close.

Once that was done, he jacked himself into the station's systems, being careful not to trigger any of the security measures put in place to stop anyone from doing exactly what he was about to do.

Fortunately for him, he was one of the people who had helped put those measures in place.

It had been a few weeks since he'd last entered cyberspace, and he indulged himself in a few glorious moments of pure freedom before getting to work. It was impossible to explain the digital world to the normals.

They were grounded in reality, where data was linear and the laws of physics held sway. When he was jacked-in, he was free in a way other beings could never be. He could soar without wings, dive into oceans of data, and change his reality with a thought or a wave of his hand.

This is what the others couldn't understand. They thought he was a freak because of his implants—a data junky who had to be protected from his own abilities. That wasn't true. It wasn't information he craved, it was the freedom. There were no rules in this place, no restrictions. Leaving cyberspace for reality was like waking from a wonderful dream and being dumped straight into an ice bath on a high gravity world. The transition sucked rocket-fumes and every movement was too slow and took too much effort.

He revelled in his few minutes of digital delight, zipping through the station's datasphere and dancing across digital rivers of information that flowed through the system like ribbons of light. As tempting as it was to stay, it wasn't safe to linger too long, so eventually he went to the digital fortress he'd built for himself inside cyberspace and got to work. A data matrix containing everything he knew about Nyx, who might have her, and where she might be located was already there within the fortress, but this time he didn't stick to authorized methods. He sent out an army of digital sprites to pry loose information from every source he could think of, every one of them capable of hacking systems and bringing down firewalls on their own. It was highly illegal technology, banned throughout the galaxy. If he was caught using it, he'd be back in a cell so fast he'd break the sound barrier.

Of course, that hadn't stopped him from hiding the software instead of handing it over when he was arrested the first time, and it wasn't going to stop him from using it now.

Once the sprites were on their way, he unplugged himself and braced for the unpleasant transition to what he thought of as 'slow-time.' *Reality. Ugh.*

After that, he packed up and went back to the team's ship, the *Malora*. It was where he spent most of his off-duty time, tucked into the cubby he'd claimed for himself. It was his workshop and office, crammed full of equipment he'd scavenged, some of it repairable, most of it only useful as spare parts for new projects. Some of those projects were not exactly Nova Force approved, so he kept those hidden and only worked on them when he knew he wouldn't be interrupted. He had plenty of other work to do in the meantime. It kept his hands and his mind engaged, and he donated the refurbished gadgets and toys he built to the only school on the station.

He was repairing a racing hover-bot when Lieutenant Commander Kurt Meyer walked up to the open doorway and rapped on the metal frame. "You got a minute?"

"Yes, sir."

There was barely room for another person in his cubby, but Kurt came inside and leaned up against the bulkhead, somehow fitting himself into the available space. "What are you working on?"

And wasn't that a loaded question. Eric opted to go with the obvious answer and hope like hell he hadn't been caught already. Kurt had an annoying ability to know far more than he should about what every member of the team was up to at any given time. Eric lifted the small bot off his worktable. "The kids sent this poor thing hurtling into one wall too many. I'm putting it back together for them, and this time I'm adding more padding, so it survives longer between repairs."

"The way Nico pilots? You might want to consider putting a forcefield around the thing."

He snorted. "I suggested that. Dante pointed out that the only way the kids will learn is if they crash and burn."

"Which says a lot about our Buttercup's upbringing," Kurt said.

"Yeah. But in Nico's case, I think he's right. Nico's clever and fearless. If he doesn't learn some restraint?" He pointed to himself. "He'll probably wind up like I did, only without my amazing charm and good looks to help him sweet-talk the judge into leniency."

Kurt rubbed his chin. "Did anyone on this team have a nice, normal upbringing?"

"Normal is a myth. Trin and Fido were raised in a hive city on Earth. What was the status quo to them would be strange to you or me. Trip's dad runs half a *fraxxing* planet, so I'm damned sure none of us could imagine what his idea of normal looks like."

"You're waxing philosophical. You only do that when you're in a good mood. Does this mean you're making progress on your side project?"

"Some. I'm close. I know I am. I just can't seem to find the last few bits of information I need to put it all together." He ran a frustrated hand through his hair. "I need to find her soon, Sabre. I've got this feeling that time is running out."

"You're not the only one feeling the pressure. Before he left for his honeymoon, Rossi spoke to Colonel Bahl. The IAF brass are looking for anything they can use to show we're still making progress against the Gray Men."

He grunted. "I was wondering when that would start." Nova Force was a specialized task force entirely focused on keeping the corporations in line. Since their team had been sent to investigate the theft of genetic material from the Vault of the Fallen, Eric and the others had been chasing a shadowy group known only as the Gray Men. They were powerful players in a game no one had even known existed, and now all of Nova Force were playing catch up.

"So, I'm asking you, Magi, how close are you?" There was something in his tone, the way he stressed Eric's nickname, that gave him pause. It wasn't one he'd earned on the team. It had come with him from his time as a lawbreaking cyber-jockey.

"I'm doing all I can, sir, but I'm up against someone

with a lot of skill, and the information I'm looking for is well hidden. There's only so much I can do without crossing any lines."

A muscle ticked in Kurt's jaw. "I see."

Eric stayed silent and waited.

"Our commander would never ask you to cross those lines."

"No, he wouldn't. And if anyone ordered me to, they'd be risking their career."

Kurt fixed him with an intent stare. "No one's ordering you to do anything."

"Good to know. I wouldn't want anyone to get into that kind of trouble."

"And nobody wants you falling into old habits. We all know what would happen if you got caught doing anything illegal." Kurt's jaw ticked again, and Eric got the unsettling feeling Kurt knew he'd already crossed the line. But if that was true, why were they having this cryptic conversation?

"I don't want to do anything that would jeopardize my life as a free man, or as a member of this team."

Kurt nodded slowly, pushed himself off the wall, and moved close enough to drop a hand onto Eric's shoulder. "We don't want to lose you, either. So, be careful. Do you understand me?"

Eric glanced at Kurt's hand, then at his XO's face. "I understand."

"Alright, then. Good talk." He squeezed Eric's shoulder then stepped back. "Oh, and a word of advice? Next time you go for a walk on the lower levels, you might want to consider wearing warmer clothes. It gets cold down there."

Son of a fraxxing *starbeast.* "Good suggestion, sir. Thanks."

"You're welcome. Don't want you getting sick. You're too important to the team. And we really need a win, soon. I think you're our best bet to get it."

He walked away without another word, leaving Eric to mull over what had just happened. He'd been caught, but instead of turning him in, Kurt was giving him unspoken permission to continue.

Next time they were at the bar, he'd have to buy him a drink.

HER ARMS BURNED, and her shoulders screamed in their sockets, but she kept going, embracing the pain. She continued doing push-ups until she reached three-hundred reps, then rose and shook her hands until the feeling returned. The floor of her cell was only a few degrees above freezing, and exercise was the only way she had to stay warm. Her medi-bots would ensure no lasting harm was done, but she was far from comfortable right now.

She raised her voice and called out to whoever was listening. "You know my rules. No grabbing. I let him keep the hand, didn't I? So why am I being punished?"

She didn't expect an answer, so when she got one, she nearly leaped out of her skin. "To remind you who is in charge. Your rules aren't rules, Subject One. They're requests that we can choose to accommodate or not."

"I have a name," she muttered.

"Which you gave yourself. Like the rules you've invented, they don't apply unless we agree to play along."

She bit back an angry retort. As tempting as it was, it wouldn't do anything except increase her misery. The owner of that smooth, cold voice had no mercy in his soul. In fact, she didn't think he had a soul at all, just an icy void full of darkness and cruelty.

"I take it from your silence that you are ceding my point?"

She gritted her teeth. "Yes, Dr. Absalom. You are correct."

He hummed in approval. "Good. Since you're in such a cooperative mood, you may have five minutes to shower, and I will end the suspension of your feeding schedule."

She knew what he wanted from her, and bile twisted in her empty stomach as she forced the words past her lips. "Thank you."

A smug little chuckle filled the room for a moment before it was cut off. She schooled her features, but she seethed with resentment. When it came time for her revenge, Absalom was at the top of her list. She'd save him for last if she could, and when his time came, she'd return every insult, hurt, and indignity he'd heaped on her, with interest.

She stripped out of her one-piece garment, removed her socks, and waited. Sometime in the next few minutes, the door to the sanitation cubby would open, and the water would come on. If she didn't move quickly, she'd lose precious seconds of her allotted time. It was yet another game they played with her, but it had been so long since she'd last had a shower, she was willing to play along this time.

She marched in place while she waited, her breath frosting around her mouth and her bare feet stinging with the cold. The heat was back on, but it would be another hour or so before things warmed up to a tolerable temperature.

When the door slid open, she sprinted through it and managed to get into position just as the first jets of water hit. It wasn't hot, but it was warm enough to drive the worst of the chill from her bones. The door slammed shut as she filled her palm with cleansing gel from the dispenser and started scrubbing, racing against time in her quest to get clean.

Her close-cropped hair only took a few seconds to wash, and she managed to get herself slathered in cleanser, scrubbed, and rinsed before the water shut off again.

There was a single small towel by the door, and she used it to dry herself thoroughly. The sanitation cubby was warm enough after the shower, but in a few seconds, she'd be back in her cell, and if she went back in wet, she'd be even colder than she'd been before.

When the door opened again, she padded over to her bed and got dressed as quickly as she could

An opening appeared in the wall, and a tray was pushed through it. Hunger clawed at her belly, and she had to fight her instinct to dive for the tray and devour the contents. Instead, she took the tray over to her bed, sat down beside it, and assessed what she'd been given. Two food tabs, a liter of water, and a cup of algae broth that had already cooled enough it was starting to congeal around the edges.

She drank the broth first and then started on the food tabs. They were dry, tasteless things that sucked the moisture out of her mouth as she ate them, but it was food, and it had been three days since she'd last been fed.

She wasn't halfway through the first tab when the headache started, and by the time she'd taken a few more bites she knew it would be a bad one. She kept eating, never letting her expression change or her movements slow. They didn't know about the headaches, or what they heralded. If they did... She didn't let herself finish that thought. She'd hidden it from them this long. She wouldn't let them learn her secret now.

She opened the connection slowly, gradually letting the cascade of thoughts and feelings flow into her.

Anger. Fear. Confusion. She sighed inwardly. Another of her clones had become self-aware.

She focused and tried to send a message to the other woman, letting her know she was not alone. Sometimes she could make them hear her. Sometimes, but not often.

"Calm." She sent the thought with as much force as she could manage. *"You are not alone."*

This time the message got through. She felt the moment the other one sensed her, their anger momentarily lessening. Questions flew at her as fast as thought, a flurry of demands she couldn't answer, all of it wrapped in a growing sense of despair.

The noise in her head grew louder, the anger exploding as the newly aware clone tried to wrestle with the knowledge of what she was and what had been done to her. Nyx took another sip of water, letting the emotions flow through her. She couldn't help them. Couldn't stop what would happen next. All she could do was bear witness.

There were only two ways this would go. Some of her clones – code-named furies - were strong enough to accept the truth and bide their time, fighting their conditioning for as long as they could, finding ways to warn their targets, and do a little good with what time they had left. They were the exception, though. For most, the knowledge that they were nothing more than tools to be used and discarded was more than their psyches could take. Those ones snapped, turning on

21

their handlers in a rabid fit of fury that had given the project its name.

This one wasn't strong enough. She shattered beneath the weight of the truth. Emotions that weren't Nyx's ripped through her, and there was no way to push through the torrent to reach the mind of her clone.

Not that it mattered. She'd seen this moment play out too many times. She knew what was coming. Fingernails bit into the flesh of her palm as she fought the need to howl in protest and rage.

The end came quickly, which was a blessing of sorts. She only caught flashes of what was happening, the scenes so jumbled she couldn't make much sense of them. There was a flash of a face twisted by fear and pain, the feel of hot blood splattering against skin, and then someone screamed a string of words she couldn't quite make out. There was a moment of shared pain, and then her mind was quiet again, the link severed.

"I will remember you," she whispered and closed her eyes, committing the moment to memory. Then, she placed that file with the others, locking it away in a part of her mind Absalom and his cohorts didn't know she had. She didn't understand it, but it was there, a repository of memories and thoughts that allowed her to retain her sense of self no matter how many times she was reprogrammed.

She finished her meal quickly, no longer hungry, but still aware that she had to eat to stay strong. She'd need all her strength soon, because with the loss of that clone, there was only one fury left. Absalom would need to create a new batch. She rose with a muffled sigh, drained the last of the water from her glass, and then placed the tray back on the floor by the slot.

Each time a new group of clones left the maturation tank, she'd become aware of them. It drained and distracted her, especially in the beginning, when they were often here on the station and there was no escaping the psychic noise and the pain that almost always accompanied the connection. She couldn't block that kind of pain, but she'd quickly become adept at hiding it.

The pain wasn't the worst of it, though. It was being teased with a vague kind of companionship. She got glimmers of insight into a world she hadn't been part of in years. The furies were her only companions, and she filed away every experience and memory they shared with her. For the ones that never gained self-awareness, there wasn't much to save, but for the rare few who managed to break their conditioning, there was more. Friendships. Laughter. Bittersweet moments made all the more poignant by the knowledge they could not last.

She went over to a metal bar affixed to the wall and started doing pull-ups, using the exercise to calm her mind and give herself something else to focus on. It didn't work. Memories assailed her, none of them hers. She let them drift through her awareness. One came back to her over and over. Laughter, and a man's face, dark eyes gleaming with desire as he leaned in to steal a kiss. It was her favorite memory, even though it was tied to a sense of longing and regret so sharp it tore at her heart.

She didn't know the man's name, only his smile, and the fact that he'd made one of her clones happy for a little while.

CHAPTER THREE

ERIC CHECKED his gear one more time, the routine of it giving his mind and hands something to do as the seconds ticked down.

They were on their way to a set of coordinates so far out that it had taken the better part of a week to get there, even with the *Malora's* engines at maximum.

Despite every precaution, there was no way to be sure that the Gray Men didn't know about this mission already. Speed was vital.

He'd wasted months already, time he'd spent trying to work through official channels, keeping on the right side of the law. Two days after he crossed the line, the information he'd been looking for started appearing. Just the occasional snippet at first, but the data kept coming in, filling in gaps and giving him new insights.

It took two more weeks to put it all together, but he knew he'd gotten it right. He'd found the base of operations for Project Fury. Somewhere on that station was Echo's batch sister, and he was going to free her.

His foot tapped out a staccato beat as he stood with the rest of his team by the airlock and waited for word from their pilot, Dante. Any second now, they'd be dropping out of stealth mode – a reflective shield that made them invisible to even the most advanced sensor arrays. If anything was going to go wrong, this was when the shooting usually started.

"Stealth mode is off, and we're on final approach. Defensive satellites appear to be deactivated." Dante's voice boomed over their comms a few minutes later.

"I told you I had those handled," Eric muttered, but he didn't activate his comms. Dante didn't need the distraction right now.

Cris chuckled. "Don't let him get to you. You know he's just trying to get under your skin."

"Yeah. Buttercup's grumpy because he has to sit this one out. You know he hates to miss a fight." Aria was checking her own gear as she spoke, strong fingers flying over every piece of equipment with a confidence born of years of practice.

"He's also got an open comm channel and can hear everything you say. Behave yourselves, or I might accidentally fly us into some turbulence," Dante said, his deep voice holding just a trace of laughter.

"Not funny, Strak. There's no turbulence in space. It's a *fraxxing* vacuum," their commander growled.

"Yeah, just like the space between Trip's ears." Aria

26

reached over to cuff the blond lieutenant on the shoulder.

"Bite me, Blink," Trip retorted.

"Why Crispin Charles Caldwell, is that an invitation?" Aria almost purred in response.

For a minute, Cris looked like he was going to say something, but he pressed his lips together and stayed quiet.

Idiot. Everyone on the team had been watching the two of them dance around each other for what seemed like forever. He'd lost good money betting that they'd have gotten together by now, but for some reason, it hadn't happened. Whatever madness had infected more than half the team, it hadn't hit them yet. It would eventually, and when that happened, he and Kurt would be the last bachelors standing.

Dax rapped his knuckles against the side of the ship. "Settle down, you lunatics, or do I have to ask Dante to pull this ship over?"

They all laughed.

"Let's go over the plan one more time." Dax pointed to Kurt. "Go."

"When we get close enough, we scan for lifeforms. Once we know where the bad guys are, we split into teams and go hunting. I'm with Blink," Kurt stated.

"Trinity is with me," Dax said.

"And Trip watches my back while I take control of the station's systems. Then we'll join the hunt," Eric added.

Dax didn't react much—he just raised one dark

brow. "That's not the plan, Ensign."

Eric raised his chin and stood his ground. "With all due respect, sir, it's not going to take me more than a few minutes to access those systems. Once that's done, I request that Trip and I take part in the main mission."

"Taking down the station's defenses and ensuring no one leaves is part of that mission," Dax replied, his tone firm.

"Yes, sir. I know, sir, but I…"

"We wouldn't be here without him, Fido. He's earned the right," Kurt said.

"He's too close to this," Dax argued.

"We've all been there." Kurt's gaze slid to Trinity, then back to Dax. The mission where the now-married pair had reunited had been a complicated one.

"He's got a point," Trin said, the corners of her mouth turned up into a smile.

Dax sighed. "Lieutenant West-Rossi, whose side are you on?"

She gave him a sharp salute and then winked. "That depends if we're in or out of uniform, sir."

Dax growled at her, straightened, and looked at Eric. "Alright. Once you've got the station secured, you and Caldwell can join us. I'll assign sectors once we have a headcount and know where everyone is."

"Yes, sir." He saluted the commander, then gave a small nod of thanks to both Kurt and Trin.

"Moving into position now. Prepare for boarding." Dante announced, and instantly everyone took their places.

"Life signs?" Dax asked.

"I've got blind spots, but…" Dante snarled a curse in Torski. "We've got incoming. There are ten life signs heading your way, moving fast."

"Get us inside now!" Dax commanded.

"That's what she said. I mean, yes, sir. Right away." Dante brought the *Malora* in against the hull of the station, and Kurt activated the boarding clamps. They slammed against the hull with a teeth-rattling clang, followed closely by the torturous hiss of cutting lasers carving into metal.

"Time," Dax barked.

"Eight seconds. Seven. Six. Five," Kurt continued the countdown. At the two-count, the *Malora's* airlock opened, and Eric tensed, adrenaline surging through his body, making everything sharper and brighter.

The hull started to fall the second the lasers finished cutting, and they were on the move before the thick slab of metal hit the deck.

The air sizzled, the metal still glowing as they passed through the newly created doorway. Alarms wailed, and the steady pulse of automated weaponfire sounded and then stopped as Trinity raised her blaster and shot out the first of the station's defenses.

His teammates fanned out and covered the hall, but he turned his back on the oncoming attackers and moved toward the nearest system access point. Cris was only two steps behind him, and Eric trusted him to watch his back.

He placed his hand on the access panel and started

his attack, deactivating anything that even looked like it might be part of the station's defenses. It was slow going, and after twenty or so seconds he snarled in frustration. "I'm going to have to go all the way in. You got this?"

Cris nodded sharply, his gaze never leaving the battle that was starting just a few meters down the hall. "Do it. Just don't fall asleep in there."

"I'll try to stay awake, can't let you bunch have all the fun," he shot back, then popped a jack into the data port in his arm and inserted the other end into the station's main system. Reality vanished, replaced by the silent and ethereal beauty of cyberspace.

Thousands of data streams flowed like quicksilver rivers, their courses unaffected by mundane concepts like gravity. Quantum helixes towered in the distance, and packets of information streaked by, lighting up the datasphere as they passed. Some of the rivers were barely more than a trickle, and there were gaps in the towers that filled the horizon, both signs there were pieces missing. He'd been expecting that. Wiping a computer system during a bugout was standard practice, but most people forgot that data was harder to eliminate than a Jeskyran roach infestation. There would be redundancies, cache files and other places where the information still resided, and he focused on finding those and shunting the contents to the *Malora's* systems via the connections he maintained with the ship.

There was something familiar about the landscape

of the place. Like he was walking through a neighborhood he'd visited before. There wasn't time to figure it out, though. He had work to do, and he set to it with glee. He altered the flow of the data streams, twisting them back on themselves, creating feedback loops that crippled the system. He disrupted systems, redirected information, and turned the elegant flow of data into a swirling vortex of chaos. The system quickly overloaded, and the automated systems crashed one by one, leaving his team with only the human defenders to deal with.

Information was everywhere, and he skimmed through it as he worked. There were no ships left on the station, and only a handful of lifeforms still onboard. He memorized their locations. One of them had to be Nyx. He wouldn't accept any other outcome.

He found the evacuation order, posted less than an hour before they'd arrived in this sector. Someone had tipped them off, but it must have been at the last minute. Whoever it was, they hadn't known about the mission until it was almost too late.

When the work was done, he withdrew from the system. His consciousness returned to reality with disorienting speed, and it took him a few seconds to adjust to the weight of reality.

"Magi, you with me?" Cris shouted and gripped his shoulder.

"I'm back. It's done."

"Yeah, I guessed that when the big bad space station stopped trying to kill us. Nice work."

Eric looked around, assessing the situation. They were alone in the corridor, and the only sounds were the distant thump of running feet and the occasional sizzle and pop from the blaster-scorched walls. There were bodies on the floor, and someone had kicked the weapons out of their dead hands before moving on.

The outer hull of the station was pockmarked and scarred from the battle. "The suicidal fools were shooting max-powered rounds? They could have punched through the *fraxxing* hull and killed us all," Eric said.

"They were screwed and they knew it. Dante says every hangar bay door is open and there's not a ship left. I'll bet you a week of galley duty that every one of those assholes has an explosive chip in his neck, same as the ones we saw on Bellex 3."

Eric shook his head and hefted his weapon. "No bet. Why worry about morale when you can just implant everyone with exploding chips and tell them to smile or have their brains splattered all over the place?"

"And there goes my appetite." Chris gave a dramatic shudder and pointed past the bodies. "The others have their targets. We're headed to level seven. Apparently, there's at least one lifeform down there, but Dante's having trouble getting a reading on it."

His intel indicated that level seven was most likely one where they were holding Nyx and any other captives. If she was still here, that was a good place to start looking. And if the Grays had taken her with them, then he'd chase them down again.

SHE WAS asleep when the evacuation alarm sounded, but Nyx was on her feet in seconds. She'd only heard that sound one other time, and she knew what it meant. They were bugging out. This was her chance.

She took up a position near the door, weight balanced, body tensed in anticipation.

The subtle hiss was so low she almost didn't hear it over the wail of the alarms. She focused on the sound, quickly realizing it was coming from the small air vents set into each corner of her cell. She took a quick, sip-like breath. There was a chemical taint to the air. She grinned fiercely. The idiots were trying to gas her.

She slowed her heart rate and breathing as much as she dared, trusting her medi-bots to deal with anything that made it into her bloodstream. Gas might work on some of the other prisoners on the station, but she was a cyborg. A fact these fools had apparently forgotten.

She waited for a handful of seconds, then let herself fall to the floor, landing with her hands beneath her, ready to launch to her feet the moment the door opened. It wasn't the plan she'd had in mind, but it would work just as well, maybe even better.

The computer's warning about security protocols became audible as the door opened. She'd heard it thousands of times in her life, but until today, no one had ever ignored it.

"She's down. Told you the gas would work."

"Better make sure," someone else said.

"Right." She watched through barely parted eyelids as the asshole nearest her hefted a stun-baton and moved closer, clearly about to light her up to test if she was truly out.

She snatched it out of his hand and leaped to her feet. "You really should have followed protocol."

"Sneaky bitch is awake!"

"*Fraxx*. Get out of there."

She flipped the baton into the air, catching it by the handle this time. While the guard's eyes were watching the baton, she lashed out with her right leg, taking him out at the knees.

He hit the deck hard and she was on him before he had a chance to recover. He glared up at her as she wrapped her hands almost tenderly around his head, the hatred in his eyes morphing into fear. She gripped hard and twisted, snapping his neck. She didn't like killing. Never had. That didn't mean she wasn't good at it.

She went for the second guard, doing a word for word recitation of the computer's recorded warning as she prowled toward him. "Alpha level security protocols have been put in place for this subject. Do not open the door until all protocols have been activated. Repeat. Do not open the door until all protocols have been activated." She raised the baton. "You should have followed instructions."

He charged her with a wild yell, brandishing his baton. She sidestepped the charge and swung her baton hard, connecting with the back of his skull. There was an audible crunch, and he dropped to the floor in a boneless heap. She paused just long enough to finish the job and search both bodies for weapons. All they carried were ident-cards, stun-batons, and an injector full of what she assumed was a sedative. She took it all. There was a cryo-pod lying open in the hall outside her cell. If they hadn't screwed up, she might be lying in that thing right now, unconscious and bound for some fresh new hell wherever Absalom and his team went next.

She'd stayed out of sight for the first while, hiding in various rooms but never staying long in one place in case they sent anyone else after her. It wasn't until the alarms went silent that she started to relax. Had they really left her behind?

She decided to take a chance and checked one of the workstations in the next room she found open. The evacuation was complete, which meant she was stuck here, at least for now.

The system showed there were still a few beings left on the station, and given that she couldn't find any reason for the evac, they had to have been left behind to protect the place from something. Or someone. She was betting on the latter, and whoever they were, they'd be coming by ship. They were her only way off this station, and she wasn't going to miss her ride.

The only good news was that the readouts showed all the station's systems were in the green. "At least I'm not going to get blown up or run out of oxygen any time soon."

She continued checking rooms along the corridor, looking for weapons or food. She didn't find either, probably because she could only open one door in five. The others required palm scans, and she didn't feel like wandering the halls carrying a severed hand. First impressions were important, and she needed to make a good one with whoever had sent Absalom and company running.

She took down two more guards as she worked her way through the station. One of them was armed with a blaster, and she happily swapped one of the batons she carried for the firearm and holster. It had been years since she'd last held a firearm, but the memory of how to use one had been encoded into her basic programming, and it only took a few seconds for her to identify the basic design and determine how it worked.

Her confidence soared as she fastened the holster around her waist.

The next time the alarms went off, she was halfway up an access ladder. The sudden noise made her miss the next rung, and she floundered for a few seconds, grateful no one was around to witness her undignified recovery.

This alarm was a call to general quarters. She grinned in anticipation. She could taste her freedom, and it was sweeter than she'd ever imagined. All she had to do now was to find a way to convince whoever was coming to take her with them when they left. Maybe if she could figure out what they were after, she could help them find it.

CHAPTER FOUR

THEY TOOK an access ladder from level to level, moving as fast as they could without taking any undue risks. The last thing Eric wanted was to get shot in the back because he'd gotten careless. Actually, that was the second to last thing. At the top of the list of things to avoid was getting his teammate shot. Not only would Cris take it personally, so would their CO, not to mention Cris' sister and her three very large, overprotective cyborg husbands.

You really think she's here?" Cris asked during a brief pause to check the hallway on this level. It was clear.

"Yes." Every scrap of evidence he'd uncovered pointed to this place, but it was more than just data. He was *sure* she was here, a gut feeling that had only gotten stronger.

Cris nodded. "Then let's find her and go home."

There was a soft sound behind them, a whisper of

fabric, nothing more, and a soft, female voice spoke in unaccented Galactic Standard. "Maybe I can help with that."

He spun around at the same time Cris did, to find himself face to face with a memory.

"Echo?"

The woman shook her head. She was armed, with a stun-baton in her hand and a blaster holstered at her hip. Her face was identical to Echo's, but she was leaner, with wary gray eyes and blonde hair cropped close to her skull. "I'm not an echo. I'm the original."

Eric slammed a lid on his emotions and tried to think logically. It wasn't easy. He'd come here looking for Echo's sister, but this... "Are you Nyx?"

Her head snapped up. "You know my name?"

He lowered his weapon and reached out to her. "You're the reason I'm here. Echo told me to find you."

Pain and shock flashed in her eyes, along with recognition. "It's you. You're the one who made her laugh."

"How do you know that?"

She took half a step forward, the hand holding the baton falling back to her side. "She sent you? How? She's dead."

How had she recognized him? Had Echo reported to her? That didn't make sense. He had so many questions, but now wasn't the time. He answered her questions instead. "She told me about you in a message she prepared before she died. She couldn't save herself, but she managed to pass on vital information to us."

"I didn't know that. I thought…" She sagged a little, then stiffened her spine and stood ramrod straight. "What's your name?"

"Eric. I'm Ensign Eric Erben, of Nova Force."

"And he's here to rescue you," Cris added, not bothering to hide his amusement.

Eric ignored the sudden impulse to shoot his teammate. Just in the foot, mind you, nothing life-threatening.

"You came all this way because one of my clones asked you to find me?"

"I came for you. My team is here because we've been tasked with taking down the Gray Men. All their projects and black sites. Everything." Eric gestured around them. "This is the home of the Fury Project, right?"

She gave him a wry smile. "Sort of."

Cris cursed. "Why sort of? What are we missing?"

She pursed her lips in thought for a long moment before answering. "I'll tell you everything I know about all this, but not until we're far away from here. When they realize they left me behind, they're going to come for me." Her hand drifted to the blaster at her hip. "I won't let that happen."

Eric let go of his weapon and stepped forward, his hand outstretched. "Tell us what you know, and I'll make sure you're protected. You have my word."

"Magi, you can't make…" Cris protested, but Eric cut him off with a slash of his hand.

"If I have to, I'll do it myself." He reached out to Nyx again. "Do we have a deal?"

She glanced at his hand, and her teeth sank into her lower lip as she considered his offer. Then, she nodded once, crossed the distance between them, and grasped his hand. "We have a deal. Echo trusted you, so I will, too."

Her touch felt so familiar he had to resist the urge to pull her into his arms and kiss her until the stormy look left her eyes and she was laughing again. But this wasn't Echo. This was Nyx, and she wasn't what he'd been expecting. "How long have you been a prisoner?"

She seemed surprised by the question. "I'm not sure exactly. Years."

He squeezed her hand, only then realizing he hadn't released his grip. "Then it's more than time you left this place. Isn't it?"

She smiled at him, a real smile that transformed her hard features into something breathtakingly beautiful. "Yes, I think it is."

Cris appeared beside him before either of them could move. "Before we go, I need to scan her."

"For what?" Eric demanded, though he managed to keep his tone respectful...mostly.

Cris gave him a level look. "Chips. Explosives. The usual."

"Right."

"I'm going to scan you, now, Nyx. It will only take a second and you won't feel a thing," Cris said, holding out the palm-sized device.

"Explosives?" She asked. "If those bastards put explosives in me I'll—" she grimaced. "Damn. I can only kill them once, can't I?"

"Afraid so." Cris barely managed to conceal a smile as he quickly ran the scanner over Nyx. "Good news, you only need to kill them the one time. No chips, no explosives."

Eric breathed a soft sigh of relief, turned, and walked back toward the ladder, still holding Nyx's hand. Somewhere behind him, Cris chuckled. "Blink is going to be sorry she missed this. I'll tell the others we found her, and we're heading back to the ship."

Eric turned to look back at the lieutenant. "Thank you." He knew he'd pushed his luck with Cris. The man outranked him, and if he forgot himself the same way with Dax, his commander would kick his ass and then bounce him out the nearest airlock. He couldn't let his desire to protect Nyx override his brain again. She wasn't Echo, and he didn't owe her anything. Once she was safe, they could both go their separate ways.

———

THE MAN whose smile had been one of her favorite memories had a name – Eric. And he'd come looking for her simply because one of her clones, a woman who had lied to him, had asked him to. She didn't know what to do with that information. Apart from the researchers who worked with Absalom and her clones, no one in the galaxy knew she even existed. This man had spoken to her and

41

seen her in a way she hadn't experienced before. It was a strange feeling. She glanced at their still-joined hands. This was turning out to be a very strange day all around.

They made the climb quickly, moving with speed and military precision from floor to floor. Both men were well trained and extremely fit for unenhanced humans. Though she wasn't sure that assessment applied to Eric. There was what looked like a data port behind one of his ears. Could he be some kind of cyborg? She didn't know, and she didn't want to ask any questions that might get her left behind.

Eric insisted on going ahead, keeping between her and any potential threat they might encounter on the way back to the ship. Not that they ran into anyone. She'd terminated the handful of guards on her level, and it appeared that Eric's team had handled the rest. She listened to the reports as they came in over their comms, putting together information until she was confident she could name every member of the team and have a good chance of identifying them on sight. There were two females and five males, one of whom was piloting their ship. Rossi was their commander, and someone she heard referred to as both Sabre and Meyer appeared to be second in command.

They were Intergalactic Armed Forces soldiers, and the star-shaped emblem on their uniforms marked them as members of Nova Force. She'd heard of them— Absalom and his team feared and despised them, which was as good a reason as any for her to trust them. The enemy of her enemy might not be her friend, but they'd make good temporary allies.

"Magi, you anywhere you can do a system check?" One of the women spoke.

"I can be in twenty seconds. What's the problem?"

"I'm in the main control room and there's a countdown in progress. Something's happening five minutes from now. I need you to ascertain what's about to happen and if we need to be gone by then."

"*Fraxx!*" Eric sprinted the rest of the way up the ladder, barely pausing to check for danger before scrambling onto the next level. She followed him, leaping the last few feet to land on the floor at his back, weapon drawn, eyes scanning the hallway.

Eric glanced back, saw her there, and gave her a wide-eyed nod. "Nice to know you've got my back."

She didn't know what to say. She hadn't fought with a team around her in years, but it was part of her programming, an instinct she'd almost forgotten. But why was she treating him like he was on her team? She shouldn't be. A handsome face and a familiar smile didn't mean he was on her side.

He turned and jogged a few meters down the hall, stopping by a data node. He slapped his open hand onto the node's shell and went utterly still. His eyes were distant and unfocused, and she realized what he was. Not a cyborg, a cyber-jockey. He'd gone into cyberspace, leaving himself completely vulnerable, trusting in her and his teammate to protect him. She looked from Eric to the blond man standing nearby. "Is he crazy? I could have killed him just now."

"You're not the first person to ask that question. I'm Lieutenant Caldwell, by the way. And if you'd tried to go after Magi, I'd have killed you." She noted with interest that the Lieutenant had an accent. There was a subtle lilt to his words that meant he was likely from the Cassien system. At least, that's what her programming indicated. It was the first time she'd actually heard anyone speak that way.

"You mean you would have tried." She bared her teeth in a grim smile. "I am very hard to kill, Lieutenant."

"Most cyborgs are," he agreed, his tone casual, but she heard the steel beneath his words.

"What do you know about my kind?" All she knew about them was what she saw through her connection to her clones. There was so much she didn't know.

"A fair bit. I've even met one of your batch-sisters. Echo."

"They're all named Echo. A cruel little joke. They were clones – echoes of the original." She tapped her chest. "Me."

"Later, I'd like to hear more about that. I'm sure our commander will, too."

"I will tell you, once we're away from here."

Eric came back to himself with an explosive curse, ending the conversation. "*Fraxx*! We need to get back to the *Malora*. Now. Go, go, go!"

They raced back to the ladder at a full sprint, with Eric repeating his warning into his comms as he ran.

"Do I want to know why we're running away, or is ignorance the way to go?" the lieutenant's tone was almost conversational.

"The sneaky sons of bitches hid a delayed command somewhere in the system code. Now it's active, I found it easily. This whole station is wired to explode. We've got less than five minutes to get to a safe distance," Eric explained.

"What is with all the explosions lately? Don't the bad guys know any other tricks?"

Once they were clear of the ladders, Nyx grabbed both the men by the hand and started running, using her strength and speed to move them faster than they could have run unaided. Eric gave her directions, and it took no time at all to reach their destination. She flew around the last corner and skidded to a stop. Two more Nova Force operatives stood a few meters in front of her, weapons up and ready to fire.

There was a tense moment, and then the dark-skinned woman and the tall, hard-eyed male with her lowered their weapons, but they didn't relax completely. "You two alright?"

"Fine, apart from the fact you nearly put a hole in my nice new uniform. Didn't you get to shoot enough things today, Jessop?" Cris asked.

"Never," the woman answered, her mouth curving into a brief, hard smile.

The man with her just rolled his eyes. "Flirt later,

you two. Get your asses on this ship before we all go boom."

"We're not flirting!" both the woman and Cris said at the exact same moment.

She glanced at Eric, who was grinning broadly. He saw her look, winked, and dropped his voice to a whisper. "They're in denial."

She didn't understand what he meant, but she nodded as if she did. Then he was leading her onboard the ship, and with a few short steps, she left her old life behind.

Freedom didn't look the way it had in her daydreams. There was no time to enjoy the moment, no chance to reflect or revel in her change of fortunes. The moment they were on board, the airlock door slammed shut, there was a metallic snick as the boarding clamps withdrew, and someone barked, "We're clear. Get us the hell out of here, Strak!"

"Hold on to something. I'm cutting power to the inertial dampeners and rerouting it to the engines." the pilot's voice boomed over the ship's speaker.

Engines rumbled to life, powerful enough to make the deck beneath her sock-clad feet shudder. Everyone scattered to take hold of something as the ship veered on one axis, then another, performing what felt like a dive.

She looked around for something to hold onto, but before she could find anything, Eric had his arm around her waist, pulling her to him with gentle strength.

She hissed in surprise and only barely managed to

stop herself from tearing herself out of his grasp. She hated being grabbed, but Eric wasn't trying to restrain her, he was helping her stay on her feet.

"Sorry," his apology stunned her even more than his assistance.

"Don't be. Just be aware that I'm used to being around beings whose primary goal was to do me harm. If you surprise me, I might not react well."

The woman who had met them at the door snorted. "Damn. Magi found another one!"

There were several chuckles and overly dramatic groans from the others.

"Another what?" she asked.

The woman leaned over so she could see her face. "Hey there, welcome aboard. I'm Lieutenant Jessop. And there's something you should know about the ensign here."

"Which is?" Nyx asked.

The man she assumed was the XO laughed. "He's got a talent for finding dangerous women."

She saw the way the others were looking at her, waiting, assessing her response. She reached up to pat Eric's arm where it curved around her waist. "Then you're right. He's found another one. In fact, I'm probably the most dangerous woman in the galaxy." She lowered her hand and looked around the crowded corridor. "You came to the station to find the Fury Project, right?"

There were several nods and another woman spoke. Her voice was firm and rang with authority, but Nyx couldn't see her from where she was. "Too bad we didn't get much before we had to abandon ship. There's still so much we don't know."

"I saved anything I thought looked interesting. It won't give us all the answers, but it might give us some idea who we're dealing with, and where they're headed next," Eric said, then gave her waist a gentle squeeze. "And we've got Nyx. She's going to help us."

"That depends on how much she knows," the unseen woman said.

Nyx straightened. "I'm happy to tell you everything I know, so long as you promise me that when you go after these bastards, I get to go with you."

The questions started flying and didn't stop until the pilot called out another warning. "The station just blew, shockwave incoming. Hold tight, this is going to get bumpy."

She could have found a handhold of her own, but she didn't. Instead, she crossed her arm over Eric's where he still held her, planted her feet on the deck, and leaned into him. Part of her knew damned well it wasn't a smart decision, but she craved human contact more than she cared to admit.

As the shockwave hit, the ship yawed and shuddered. There were grunts as they were thrown against the bulkhead, but Eric never let go of her, keeping his body between hers and the hard walls of the ship as chunks of the station slammed into their shields. It didn't last long, but she spent those seconds looking at Eric, comparing the man holding her to the handful of memories she'd gleaned from her clone.

He had black hair long enough to show some curl, though it was shorter than her recollections of him. His face was leaner, too, but his eyes were the same. The brown of his irises were so dark they looked almost black in the dim light. She'd already gotten a look at his body, but feeling it pressed against hers gave her a greater appreciation. He was all lean, hard muscle beneath his uniform, but despite his strength, he held her carefully, as if she were someone worth protecting.

Once the ship leveled off again, he loosened his hold, and she turned to face him.

"You good?" he asked.

"Yes." Then a phrase she hadn't spoken in ages came to mind and she belatedly added, "Thank you."

"You're welcome." Their gazes met, and for a second, she thought he might lean in and kiss her. The idea unleashed a disorienting flood of emotions, and she stepped away.

He let her go, and she caught a flash of guilt in his dark eyes as he did so. "Sorry. You look so much like her."

"I understand. You seem familiar to me, too."

"Which is something I don't understand. How can I be familiar to you? We've never met."

"We've got a lot of questions for you, Nyx. I'd like to get started hearing the answers."

"Of course." She looked over to the man speaking. He had dark hair, piercing blue eyes, and an air of command. "And once you agree to my terms, I'll be happy to answer all your questions. Believe me, no one wants to destroy these people more than I do."

"You want to be part of any team that moves against them," Rossi stated. It wasn't a question.

"I do." She met his gaze and waited. If he turned her down, then she'd have to guard what she knew until she could find someone who would give her what she wanted.

After a few seconds, he rapped his knuckles against the bulkhead and nodded. "I can't make any promises, but if that's the price for taking these people down, then you'll have my support."

"Thank you, Commander Rossi."

He gave her a ghost of a smile. "Listening in on our communications, were you?"

"Of course." She glanced around at the rest of the team, then started pointing to each of them in turn. "Meyer, your XO. Lieutenants Caldwell, Jessop, and West-Rossi. And your pilot is named Strak, though I did not catch his rank."

"Buttercup's a Master Sergeant," Eric informed her.

"And you've already met Ensign Erben," the commander said. "Magi, show our guest to the main briefing room. We'll join you shortly. I need to report to command and let them know we're on our way back." His expression darkened. "And that someone tipped off the target to our arrival. How long ago did they leave, Nyx?"

"The evac alarm went off less than an hour before you arrived."

"Small blessings. If they'd had longer, we wouldn't have found as much as we did, and I'm betting we wouldn't have found you, either."

She shook her head. "I killed the ones who came for me. They were in a rush and made mistakes. It cost them."

Everyone stared at her for a second and then Lt. Jessop laughed. "I like her already."

The blond man rolled his eyes. "Of course you do. She's even scarier than you, Blink."

"And on that note, everyone to their stations. We'll debrief in thirty minutes," Rossi said and everyone moved at once.

Everyone but Eric. He stayed where he was, and so did she. Once they were alone, he pointed down the corridor. "Briefing room is this way. We can grab you some food and something to drink on the way."

Her stomach growled at the mere mention of food. "That would be appreciated."

He tossed his next question over his shoulder as he walked in the direction he'd indicated. "Alright then. Burgers, pizza, or are you a dessert first kind of woman?"

"Since I've never eaten any of those, I honestly have no idea."

Eric stumbled as he tried to stop, turn, and stare at her simultaneously. "What do you mean, you've never had any of them?"

"Prisoner and research subject, remember?"

"But you weren't always a prisoner, were you?"

She'd never had to say the words before. Everyone in her world had known what she was. "I've never been anything else."

Eric's mouth fell open, and she tried not to flinch away from the horror and pity she saw in his eyes. "What? Never?" he asked.

"I'll explain when everyone else joins us. No sense going through it all twice." Her stomach growled again.

He shook his head and seemed to regain his train of thought. "Right. Food now, talk later. Come on, the galley's just a few doors down."

She fell in behind him and surprised herself when she let her gaze drop to the snug fit of his uniform across his ass.

Not happening.

She had a long list of wrongs to avenge, and getting distracted by anything, or anyone, was not on the agenda.

CHAPTER FIVE

Eric knew that Nyx was one of the most dangerous, capable beings he'd ever encountered. Too bad logic had taken a back seat to his sudden, primal urge to take care of her.

"Would you like me to show you how to use a food dispenser? Or are you familiar with this kind of tech?"

She pressed her lips together and stared at the machine. It was obvious that she didn't know how to use it, and equally clear she didn't like not knowing.

"I can figure it out, but it would probably be faster if you showed me."

He kept his explanations brief, showing her the basic operating controls and the expansive menu of food and drink options. It was the way she stared at the menu that twisted his heart. There was moment of disbelief and wonder that she quickly hid behind an impassive mask, but he'd seen it. It was as if she couldn't quite accept that it was all real. Not just the choices, but the fact she was free to make them.

"Your first meal as a free woman definitely needs to include dessert. I'm thinking chocolate ice cream. What else would you like to try?"

She waved her hand at the screen, then grinned at him. "All of it."

"How about we start with some of the crews' favorites? A burger, a couple of slices of pizza, and lasagna—you're going to love that."

She made the selections as he suggested them, adding several of her own, as well.

"Oh, and the ice cream," she said.

"I think you're going to need some apple pie, too. It's my favorite."

"Then I definitely need to try that."

It would take the dispenser a few minutes to prepare their orders, so Eric moved over to another station, one programmed for beverages only. This time, he made the order himself, requesting one of the items he'd programmed in himself. Two mugs of steaming cocoa appeared a minute later, both of them topped with whipped cream and scented lightly with cinnamon. He handed one to her and raised the other in salute.

"Welcome to freedom, Nyx."

She raised her mug in an action that mirrored his own. "Thank you. I…" she looked around, and for a moment he saw past her armor to the vulnerable and uncertain woman beneath. "I'm still trying to come to terms with it all."

"Chocolate will help. Trust me." He took a sip of his cocoa, then watched as she tried her first taste.

She took the smallest sip, then made a small coo of pleasure so sexy it sent a surge of blood straight to his cock. He watched, mesmerized as she drank more of the cocoa with obvious enjoyment. She drained the mug in one go, and when she moved her hand away, she had whipped cream smeared across her upper lip, and there was a little on the tip of her nose.

His brain short-circuited, leaving him staring as she swiped the froth away with her tongue, doing it just slowly enough he wondered if she was aware of how tempted he was to do something stupid, like kiss away the last traces of the rich foam.

"You've got a little uh… there." He touched the tip of his nose and inwardly congratulated himself for resisting temptation. Then she broke him again by running her forefinger down her nose, then licking the cream from her finger.

"Gone?"

"All gone." His voice was so rough it sounded like it had been dragged across sandpaper.

"Could I have another one? That was delicious. What was it called, so I can order it again?"

He cleared his throat and willed his brain to start working again. "Of course. You can have whatever you —I mean, as many as you like. The galley is fully stocked. It's listed under my name, see?" He pointed to the menu, which included personal favorites for each of the crew. "It's the cocoa with whipped cream option."

She held the mug up. "What do I do with this?"

"Put it in there. The computer will run a cleaning cycle once the unit is full."

She put the mug into the cleaning unit, then requested another cocoa from the dispenser. She bounced on the balls of her feet while she waited for it to finish making the drink, and had the fresh mug in her hands less than a second after the whipped cream was added. "So good. I mean it. I had no idea. Sometimes I got flashes of experiences from the others, but all I felt was their enjoyment, not the sensation itself."

A thought struck him, and he knew the answer even as he asked the question. "Flashes? Is that how you recognized me back on the station?"

She nodded, suddenly cautious again. "It is. I sometimes see things. Impressions mostly. The people who held me didn't know about that. I kept it from them. They tore me apart trying to understand why I was different, but I managed to keep that hidden."

"You saw me with Echo."

"Only bits and pieces, but yes. I know you were kind to her."

"Uh, yeah. I didn't know her long, but I liked her." He finally remembered his own drink and took several more sips, buying himself a little time to organize his thoughts. Finding Nyx had been important to him because it was a way of honoring Echo's memory. But now she was here, he didn't feel like he was doing this for Echo anymore.

"She liked you, too." Nyx tipped her head to one side and the slightest hint of pink stained her cheeks. "None of the others ever felt that way about anyone. At least, not that I knew of. You were special."

"So was she."

Nyx uttered a soft sigh. "They all are — were," she corrected herself and hoped he didn't catch her slip. For now, she intended to keep the existence of the last free fury a secret. If she could connect to her, she might be able to track her down, and the last time they'd connected, that fury had been with Absalom. It was a thin chance, but it was the only chance she had.

The conversation faded into silence, but before it turned awkward, the food dispenser beeped, announcing that the first of her meals were ready. They still had a little time, so he helped her carry the dishes to the table. It was little more than a long sheet of scratched and dented steel, and like the chairs around it, created to be practical and sturdy, not comfortable.

Most civilians would have complained about the lack of padding, but Nyx claimed a seat without comment. It was another reminder that she wasn't like most people he knew.

She looked from dish to dish for several seconds, took one of the fries off the plate, dipped it in ketchup, and tried a bite. After a few seconds, she swallowed, her expression unreadable.

He sat across from her, curious to see her reactions to the rest of her feast. After the fries, she worked her way through every dish on the table. Her expression didn't change much, but he could tell that she was enjoying herself. She tackled the dishes with enthusiasm, and couldn't quite suppress her occasional moans of pleasure as she discovered something she truly liked. Those moans made him grateful he was sitting, because listening to her delightful little sounds of pleasure kept his cock in a constant state of arousal and filled his imagination with thoughts he had no business having about a woman he'd just met.

She hadn't gotten to dessert before they had to go, so he gathered the remains of her meal and put it on a tray to take with them. She was clearly starving, and this wasn't likely to be a short meeting.

"We don't have long, but there's a sanitation room on the way if you want to use it. I'll take the food to the briefing room and come back for you."

"Thank you, yes." She paused before following him back into the corridor. "Are you allowed to leave me unsupervised?"

"You're not a prisoner, Nyx. If you're not supposed to be somewhere, the door won't open. Otherwise, you're free to wander." He gave her a wry grin. "Besides, you're a *fraxxing* cyborg. If you decided to do something, I'd have a hell of a time stopping you."

"You're the reason I'm free right now. Why would I turn on you?"

He answered before his brain could filter the words coming out of his mouth. "I never would have believed Echo could turn on her friends, but she did."

Nyx's expression turned stony and her next words

were jagged and raw. "I'm not like my clones. I was never like them. I broke my conditioning within weeks, and nothing they did to me reactivated it. I was a puzzle they couldn't solve, but they never stopped trying." She gave him a look as fierce and primal as anything he'd ever seen. "They never controlled me. Everything I did was my choice. So, if I turn on you, it's because I chose to."

He should probably have said something calming, or thoughtful, or at least carefully considered. Instead, he went with his strength – smartassery. "Note to self, don't piss off the badass cyborg. I'm way too cute to die."

She blinked at him, her mask still in place but her gray eyes were full of surprise. "You…uh…"

"You're speechless, huh? I sometimes have that effect on women."

The chill left her expression and the corners of her mouth lifted in a tiny smile. "I was right about you. You're insane."

"But cute. Don't forget cute. Hang on, when did you decide I was insane?"

"The moment you jacked into cyberspace and left yourself vulnerable to a cyborg you'd only just met. I could have killed you, Eric."

He finally gave into temptation, shifting the tray to one hand so he could touch her cheek gently with the other. "But I knew you wouldn't."

"I'm not your Echo. You don't know me." She met his gaze but didn't move away from his touch.

"You're not Echo," he agreed, tracing the line of her jaw with his fingertips. "But I don't believe she would have sent me to find you if she thought you'd kill me. If she wanted me dead, she could have done it herself."

"That's true enough." She moved her head, breaking their connection. "You're really not afraid of me?"

He dropped his hand back to the tray he carried and shook his head. "Like Blink said, I have a thing for dangerous women. And you might be the most dangerous woman I've ever met. So no, I'm not afraid of you, Nyx."

She gave him a ghost of a smile. "Which proves that you really are insane."

THE REALIZATION that her clone had sent a crazy man to find her was amusing, but it made a certain amount of sense, too. A sane, practical being would never have considered doing what Eric had, putting together the pieces and tracking her down. She couldn't begin to imagine how he'd done it at all, but she was grateful that he had.

He left her to wash up, promising to be back in a few minutes. She went through the door he indicated and was immediately struck by a view she hadn't seen clearly in years – her own face. The last time she'd had access to a mirror she'd broken it and armed herself with the shards. Since then, she'd only seen her reflection in the polished metal of her shower, or in the water of her sink.

The jumpsuit she wore was a washed-out gray and it hung off her frame, distorting the lines of her body and making her look even taller than her six-foot height. Her face was all hard lines and angles, though there was a hint of softness to her mouth.

She could still remember the touch of Eric's fingers along her jaw. She liked the way he touched her. More than she wanted to. He wasn't part of her mission. She needed to tell these people what she knew and make sure she was with them when they went after the ones who had hurt her. She owed Absalom and the others a painful death, and by all the stars that burned, she was going to give it to them.

She ran the water, as hot as she could stand, and used generous globs of cleanser gel to wash up. It lathered into a rich, luxurious foam that tingled on her skin and smelled amazing. When she was done, she dried herself with one of a small stack of towels set beside the sink. They were soft and absorbent, wicking away the moisture from her skin in mere seconds. It struck her that this simple room held more luxury than she'd experienced in her entire life, and for the first time she wondered how she'd adjust to it all. She chased that thought away with a firm reminder that none of it really mattered. Creature comforts were a distraction from the final goal - revenge.

She finished up and rejoined Eric. He was leaning

against the wall across from the door, his arms folded across his chest in a casual pose. "Better?" he asked.

"Much better. I don't know what it was, but I really liked the smell of the soap."

"Mint…something. Spearmint, maybe. If you like it, I'll make sure the sanitation cubby in your quarters gets stocked with it."

It took a second for his words to register. "My quarters?"

He pushed off the wall, giving her a cocky grin as he walked past her. "Well, yeah. Where did you think you'd be sleeping? We won't be back to our base on the Drift for days."

"I honestly hadn't thought about it."

"This ship has guest quarters. The commander will assign you some after the debrief. Like I said, you're not a prisoner, Nyx. Those days are over."

It was a short walk down the hall to another door. This one led into a briefing room. It was larger than the galley, but not by much. The table was metal again, but the chairs placed around it were padded. There was a holographic projector embedded in the center of the table, though it was deactivated at the moment. There were screens on all four walls, all of them showing various starscapes, likely the views from outside the ship.

The tray with her food had been set in front of a chair positioned at the center of the rectangular table. She took her seat, and Eric claimed the one across from her. She noticed that it was the one that controlled the projector. She'd assumed that would be the commander's seat, and she relaxed a little as she realized that she'd be able to see him during this meeting instead of having to stare at Commander Rossi.

She didn't have any illusions about what would happen now. They were going to grill her for information, checking and double-checking her story, wringing out every detail she could remember. Given that she was a cyborg with perfect recall, that was going to take some time.

The others arrived in the next few minutes, pouring glasses of water with actual ice cubes floating in it from the pitchers set on the table. They eyed her food with interest, but no one said anything about it as they introduced themselves by name and rank and took their seats.

She kept eating, though she tried to hide her enjoyment of each new taste. The ice cream was delicious, melting into silken decadence on her tongue. She was about to try the apple pie when a massive male entered the room, his size alone indicating that he wasn't entirely human. He filled the doorway and had to duck his head as he passed through. When he raised it again, he was smiling at her, showing her a flash of his fangs. Torski, then. At least in part.

"We're bringing snacks to these meetings, now? Good plan." He settled himself at one end of the table and gave her a friendly nod. "I'm Master Sergeant Dante Strak. You must be Nyx."

"I am." She considered for a minute, then pushed

the plate with several slices of pizza on it down his way. "Pizza?"

"Thank you." Dante snagged a piece with a nod.

"Just don't offer him a hamburger," Eric told her in a loud stage whisper. "He's still got issues about those."

Dante growled, but she didn't sense any real animosity behind the sound. "What did I tell you about mentioning those *fraxxing* things, Magi?"

"Food poisoning?" she asked.

There was muffled laughter from all around the table. "Dante got sent undercover and ended up on his own for a few days…with limited food choices. He survived mostly on lizard burgers."

"Still better than a steady diet of food tabs and algae broth," she said.

Several of the team groaned and shuddered. "Is that what they fed you?" Trinity asked.

"Nothing but. This is the first time I've had real food," Nyx gestured to the remains of her feast.

"Then we're going to have to find a way to kill them twice. That's got to be against the laws of the Unified Galactic Agreement," Cris said.

"No killing without authorization. Definitely not if you're going to try and kill anyone twice," Commander Rossi walked into the room. His gaze landed on her and her food and he smiled a little. "Good. Ensign Erben saw to it you had what you needed."

He dropped into his chair at the head of the table and steepled his fingers in front of him. "This entire meeting is being recorded, starting now." He glanced at

Eric, who tapped his keyboard a few times and then nodded to him.

"I'd like for you to start by giving us your name and serial number, please," the commander asked.

She took a quick sip of water before speaking. "I am Subject One, serial number four-seven-three-eight-two-two-six-nine-Alpha-seven-five. I'd prefer to be called Nyx."

"Alright, Nyx. What corporation created you?"

"I was created by Astek Corporation."

No one actually spoke, but there was a collective murmur of surprise from everyone around the table.

"Astek? I thought they were one of the good guys," Aria said.

Dante uttered a short, cynical bark of laughter. "We're the only good guys I know of."

Her experience might be limited, but Nyx had to agree with the big male. Over the years she'd met various beings from different corporations, races, and loyalties, and very few of them could be described as decent, never mind good.

Dax ignored the comments and continued his questions. "When were you created?"

"I don't know the actual date, but it was at least a year before the war ended. I heard references to it at the time, though much of it didn't make sense until later." She sat back in her chair and squared her shoulders. "This might go faster if I just give you my background all at once instead of answering questions."

Dax nodded, a flicker of approval in his expression. "By all means."

"I was created by Astek. I was designed to be an infiltration unit and assassin, but I was pulled after my first mission, when my handlers identified a flaw in my programming." She smiled a little as she recalled the absolute panic that had ensued when she'd defied her first order. "The behavioral conditioning and systemic programming they used to control us didn't work on me."

"You broke the conditioning that early? It took most cyborgs years to do that. How'd you manage it?" Eric asked.

"I didn't *break* it. I'm more or less immune. It just took me time to realize that I was following orders because I didn't know what else to do, while everyone else was doing it because they had no choice. When I was ordered to accommodate the sexual needs of one of the human techs, I refused. When he insisted. I resisted. Strenuously. After that, I was locked away and never saw my batch siblings again. In fact, the only cyborgs I saw after that were test subjects like me, and most of those were my clones – copies created by Absalom as part of his research into my unique condition."

"You came out of the maturation tanks completely self-aware? I thought that couldn't happen," Eric said.

"It isn't supposed to. No one knows how or why it happened. I was handed over to a group of scientists and researchers, led by a smart, powerful man who wanted to figure out why I was resistant. At the time, they thought I was the only one who gained full autonomy. They didn't know there were others until the war ended and the cyborgs revealed themselves."

"But once they knew, why didn't they just release you with the others?" This time the question came from Trinity.

Rage streaked through her. Not the hot, wild fury of battle. This feeling was as cold as the dark expanse outside the ship, an icy intent sharpened to a deadly edge over the years. She fisted her hands on the table and uttered her next words through gritted teeth. "Because Dr. Jules Absalom is a heartless bastard, and he isn't one to relinquish his toys."

The room erupted into chaos. Questions flew, voices were raised, and Trinity rose to her feet to start pacing behind her chair.

After a few seconds, the commander rapped his knuckles sharply on the tabletop, and the room fell into almost instant silence. "Dr. Jules Absalom was on the station with you? The station we just left?"

"He was. He oversaw Project Fury. He isn't there all the time though, he moves from lab to lab, overseeing various projects. And before you ask, I don't know what they were, or where he went. I only knew what I was told, or what I could learn for myself."

Dax nodded. "Was he there today?"

"I don't think so, no." She considered things for a few seconds, then added. "If he had been there, the guards that came for me wouldn't have been sloppy and skipped the protocols. He doesn't tolerate those kinds of mistakes. I take it you know who he is."

Dax nodded. "We've encountered his influence before."

Eric shifted forward in his chair. "Did you have any contact with the AI that ran the station?"

"Not really. It wouldn't interact with me for obvious reasons. Apart from a few set statements I never even noticed it. Why?"

Dax ignored her question and asked another one of her. "What about the name V.I.D.A?"

She searched her databanks and memories but came up blank. "I've never heard that name before."

"But that doesn't make sense, V.I.D.A. is Absalom's greatest—" Eric's comment died midsentence when Dax raised his hand and fixed the other man with a hard stare.

"She's not been cleared for that information, Ensign."

"She's probably a better source of information about Absalom than anyone else in the galaxy, sir."

"I don't disagree with you on that point, Magi, but this is only the first step, and there are rules we need to follow." Dax's tone softened slightly, and she noticed the way he switched from using Eric's rank to his nickname. It was the first time she'd seen someone lead that way. *Interesting.*

Eric didn't look happy, but he didn't say anything else.

Dax turned his attention back to her. "What else can

you give us? Names? Descriptions? We've been playing catch up too long, and I'm sick of it. Give us the information we need to find these shadow-dwelling bastards, and I will do all in my power to make sure you're with us when we take them down."

"Do I have your permission to interface with your computer system?" It was a delicate question, and the answer would give her an idea how much they trusted her, or at least, how much they needed the information she had.

"Why?"

She put a tick in the "don't trust me too much column" and inclined her head to the projector. "I'm a cyborg. Many of my memories are recorded data. I can give them to you."

Dax's eyes widened. "All of them? Just like that?"

"Most of them," she corrected him, keeping her tone level. "But I will give you everything about Absalom, his team, and the Fury Project."

His lips thinned and his brows knitted, but after a moment he nodded. "Trust works both ways, I suppose."

She allowed herself a small smile as she rose to her feet. "First steps."

Nyx walked around the table until she was standing at Eric's shoulder. He shifted slightly in his chair, giving her room enough to reach past him to the machine set into the table.

"Give me a moment to set this up. I'm creating a secure data cache to contain whatever you give us."

"While making sure I don't have access to anything else? I know you're going to do it anyway, but believe me, it's not necessary." She touched his shoulder. "My talents are very different from yours."

He flashed her a grin. "Nice to know you've already noticed how talented I am."

Aria snorted in amusement. Cris groaned and then muttered, "You just can't help yourself, can you?"

"Nope, I can't. I've learned to embrace my truth. You should try it sometime, Your Lordship," Eric shot back, his fingers flying over the console in front of him.

Kurt slapped a big hand down on the table. "We're still being recorded, remember? Behave or I'll kick both your asses so hard you'll be tasting the polish on my boots for days."

"Yessir. Sorry, sir."

The pair spoke in perfect synch, and she had to stifle an urge to laugh. It was obvious they'd done this often enough that the response was automatic. She hadn't been with her batch-siblings for long, but there had been moments like this with them. She hadn't thought about it for years. Hadn't thought about *them* in years.

She buried the memories, and the pain that accompanied them, and forced herself to focus on the here and now. She pressed her hand over one of the machine's data ports and let the information flow out of her. Every name. Every face. Every detail she'd gleaned from half-heard conversations, glimpses of monitors, and the vague impressions and thoughts her clones had sent to her over the years.

She gave them everything she'd agreed to, and when it was done, she withdrew her hand from the data port and let it rest on Eric's shoulder. "Show it to them."

The air in the middle of the table shimmered. Then, images and data files began to appear on it, dozens, then hundreds, then thousands. Eric moved his hands, one settling over the data port she'd used, the other flipping the projected images, sorting and arranging them faster than her eyes could track.

When he was done, a single image floated in the center of the table, larger than the others. The man in the image was somewhere in his early thirties, with dark, lank hair and a hawkish nose. Even in the picture, his eyes were cold and there was a hint of cruelty in the lift of his mouth.

Eric looked at her quizzically. "According to the metadata, that's Absalom. But it can't be."

"It can, and it is," she said.

"Jules Absalom is over sixty years old. That man can't be more than thirty." Dax said.

Another picture appeared beside the first one. They were almost identical, though the man in the second picture was older. There were lines etched around his eyes and mouth, and silver threaded through his thinning hair. "That's the last image we have of the doctor, before he disappeared," Eric said.

"He's got a twin? A son?"

The commander's voice rose above the others. "The sonofabitch cloned himself."

Nyx's stomach twisted at the idea that her tormenter had copied himself. How many of him were out there?

She didn't realize she'd spoken her question out loud until Eric reached up to touch her hand where it rested on his shoulder. "It doesn't matter how many there are, Nyx. We're going to find them all and bring them to justice. It's what we do."

She nodded, grateful for his words, even though she knew it wouldn't be enough. She didn't want justice. She wanted blood.

CHAPTER SIX

ERIC DIALED up the speed on the treadmill and lengthened his stride yet again, trying to ignore the metaphor of running full tilt while still going nowhere. The frustration Eric had felt trying to locate Nyx was nothing compared to the new levels of vexation he'd discovered in the two weeks since he'd found her.

Dante wandered into view, a towel draped over one powerful shoulder and a grin on his face. "Are you trying to burn off that nutritional abomination you called lunch, or is there some deeper reason you're trying to hit light speed on that thing?"

"It was a fruit compote with a serving of protein."

Dante snorted. "It was pie and ice cream. For lunch. With not a vegetable to be seen. You eat like my kid wishes he could."

He slowed the treadmill to cool-off speed. Dante was clearly here to talk. "It was delicious, and I hadn't eaten today. I've had too much to do. In fact, I can't chat long. I need to get back to work. That data isn't going to review itself."

The big man folded his arms and growled. "Not until we talk."

"You drew the short straw this time, huh?" He kept walking and didn't bother looking at Dante. He knew what was coming. He'd heard the speech more than once since they'd gotten back to Astek station. The brass didn't want him to have contact with Nyx. They said it was because they needed to be sure she wasn't a plant, but that wasn't the whole story. He wasn't even allowed to ask her questions about the data they'd recovered. Any inquiries he wished to make were to be submitted in writing and were answered the same way.

She wasn't the only one they were worried about.

"No. I volunteered." Dante slapped the control panel and the treadmill shut down with short stream of alarmed little beeps. "And you need to listen to me, Magi."

"Is that an order?" He knew he was being an asshole, but he couldn't seem to stop himself lately. It was probably a good thing he hadn't seen Nyx in person—it had saved him from adding her to the list of people he'd snarled at since they'd gotten back. Of course, he hadn't exactly been out of contact, either. But talking to her on the sly wasn't the same as being face to face.

"Of course it's not an order—you outrank me. You done being an ass, now?"

Eric raised his hands and stepped off the machine. "Yeah. Sorry."

Dante tossed him the towel. "I get it. They're not treating her right, and they're acting like your judgment can't be trusted for shit. If it were me, I'd be pissed, too."

"I thought I'd proven myself, shown I was loyal, that I could keep on the right side of the law. Turns out, none of that matters." He looked up at Dante. "I'm beyond pissed right now, but that's no excuse for taking it out on you or the rest of the team. I know you all still trust me. So, for what it's worth, I'm sorry." He scrubbed the towel over his face, head, and neck, and tossed it into an open laundry chute. "Now, if you're not here to remind me to keep my nose clean and stay away from Nyx, what are you here to talk about?"

"You. You're pushing yourself too hard. You're not going to be any good to anyone the rate you're going." Dante looked at the treadmill pointedly. "These things take time. We'll find these bastards."

"And when we do, do you think they'll trust Nyx enough to let her come with us? They won't even let her move around the *fraxxing* station right now. We didn't free her, we just upgraded her to a nicer prison." And that was what was really bothering him. The investigation was grinding along slowly, but he was used to that. The way they were treating Nyx, though? It wasn't right. An IAF battle cruiser had met them on the way back to the Drift, and they'd had orders to transfer her to the larger ship for the duration of the trip home. None of them liked it, but orders were orders.

He'd only been able to stay in contact with her because he'd taken steps.

She was being interrogated and examined almost daily, her activities restricted to the point she couldn't leave her quarters inside Nova Force HQ. Scientists and medical experts came and went, and no one would let him so much as talk to her. If he hadn't found a way around the restrictions, she'd probably hate him by now.

Dante grunted. "No argument there. Come on, you still need to work out some of that anger you're carrying. I'll grab the pads and meet you on the mats."

"I should really get back to work." He had been systematically parsing through every bit of code he'd recovered from the station they'd raided. It was tedious work, but he'd uncovered a few key bits of data that fit nicely into the framework Nyx's information had created.

"We're not done talking yet. Get your ass to the mat. I haven't seen you practice your hand-to-hand for weeks."

"Been busy kicking digital ass." He toed off his shoes and socks and crossed over to the sparring area. He grabbed a pair of smart-fit gloves and held them to his hands, keeping them still until the fabric had wrapped itself around his fingers in a snug, supportive fit. He flexed his hands a few times and the nanite-enhanced material made a few minor adjustments. By the time Dante strolled over to join him, he was ready to go.

"You need to keep up your combat skills." Dante looked serious for a moment. "Don't give them any reasons to question your place on this team."

He threw a few light punches at Dante's raised hands before answering. "You think it's like that?"

"I think we'd be stupid to assume it wasn't. Trust is in short supply right now. They wanted a win, and we gave 'em one, but it came with more questions than answers. Fido's grumpy from all the meetings he's been dragged into, and Sabre's not much better. On top of all the politics and paranoia, someone leaked the details of our mission to the enemy. The commander says they're going through everyone's records with a *fraxxing* microscope."

Eric threw another fast flurry of punches, then stepped back. "Including us? We're the ones whose mission was compromised. That doesn't make any sense."

Dante snorted. "Common sense is not a requirement to get promoted to command. In fact, I'm pretty sure they consider it a detriment."

He grinned. "That would explain a lot."

They fell into a familiar rhythm, Eric throwing combinations of punches and kicks, his speed increasing along with the force of his blows as they talked. Dante was right, he needed this—both the exercise, and the chance to talk.

"How's it coming? The stuff you're working on?"

"Slow. I found a few more pieces today. They'll be part of our next briefing. Nothing planet-shattering, but it verifies some of what Nyx told us. I recovered part of a duty roster, shift rotations, work assignments, that kind of thing. All the names match up. I'm running a check of all databases we have access to, trying to find more about these people, but so far it's a big blank."

"Like Everest?" Dante referred to one of the Gray's lackeys, now deceased thanks to an explosive chip in his neck. He'd been in their custody when he died, and all they'd learned about him was that he was a clone, and a ghost whose entire life was a work of elaborate fiction.

"I think so, yeah. So, either the Gray Men are creating an entire workforce of clones, or they've managed to delete all those people's entire records from existence. I'm not sure which of those things worries me more."

"Everything about that bunch worries me. They've got enough power and influence to do anything they want, and we still don't know what their endgame is. Rossi is right. We're playing catch up, and I think we're running out of time to figure it out."

"Nyx is helping with that. Or she was. If I were her, I'd be seriously reconsidering how much help I'd give the people who promised her freedom and then treated her like a prisoner." He slammed the pads with a powerful kick. "It's not right."

"You like her, don't you?" Dante's question threw

him off his stride and he almost missed landing his next punch.

"What? No. I mean yeah, she seems nice enough." He struggled to recover from both the physical and verbal flailing he had going on.

Dante, the smug bastard, laughed at him. "That's what I thought."

His next set of blows landed with the full force of his frustration behind them, and Dante had to take a step back to compensate. "Like it matters either way. If the brass has it their way, I'm never going to see her again."

"Oh, ye of little faith. Sometimes things work out, you know."

He threw another punch. "Not in my experience."

"I know. But you're forgetting something."

"What's that?" He ripped through another flurry of blows and finished with a high kick that made a satisfying smack when it landed.

"You've got friends." Dante raised one of the pads in a wave of greeting. "Nice to see you again, Nyx."

It had to be a trick. He hadn't even heard the gym door open. He spun around anyway, hope overtaking reason for a second. Nyx was standing by the door with Trinity, and holy *fraxx*, did the cyborg look good.

He'd introduced her to every dish the ship's food dispenser could create on the trip back, and she'd apparently continued to eat well, because she was almost glowing with health and vitality. The shadows beneath her eyes were gone, and there was a fullness to her face and body that hadn't been there before. She was dressed in workout gear - a dark blue pair of loose-fitting pants and a tank-top emblazoned with the Nova Force emblem, a silver five-pointed star.

He was halfway across the room before he even noticed his feet were moving. "You're here." He winced at his suave statement of the obvious and tried again. "You look good."

"They agreed to let me out of my gilded cage if I agreed to wear this." She raised her arm, showing him the simple band of flat, gray metal encircling her wrist. He recognized it – a tracker. He'd worn an identical one all through IAF basic training and his probation period with Nova Force.

"I'm sorry."

He'd already apologized to her more than once during their secret conversations, but this was the first time he'd gotten to say it to her in person.

"This is not your fault." She glanced over at Trinity. "Or yours. I appreciate what you and your husband did."

"This was not how any of us expected things to go." Trinity looked like she wanted to say a lot more but held her tongue. It was a skill that every officer seemed to learn eventually. Everyone but him.

"You and Rossi shouldn't have to have done anything at all. This is all kinds of *fraxxed* up." He took a breath and fought through his anger. "But I appreciate what you two did. However you managed it. I owe you."

"I'll remind Dax about that the next time the

Malora's engines need recalibrating." Trin turned to Nyx. "I need to speak to the sergeant for a moment. You go ahead and check out the equipment. Magi, give her the tour, will you?"

"Yes, ma'am. I'd be happy to." And the next time they were out for drinks, he owed his entire team a round. Dante was right, he should have trusted his friends to have his back and make things right.

He looked at Nyx and gave her a small smile. "You look like you came here to work off some frustration. Where would you like to start?" Whatever she wanted to do, he was game. Run. Weights. He'd even spar with her if she wanted, despite the fact she could probably put him in traction without breaking a sweat. In fact, the idea of getting tangled up and sweaty with Nyx was really damned appealing, and now that she was here, he couldn't remember any of the reasons he was supposed to stay away from her.

───────

WHEN TRINITY HAD SUGGESTED she come to the gym to work out, Nyx had agreed without hesitation. She'd learned how to use weight machines and treadmills on the *Malora*, and she'd missed the opportunity to rebuild her strength and test her limits since she'd been transferred to another ship and confined to quarters. It hadn't occurred to her that Eric would be here today, and she'd enjoyed watching him work out against

Dante before the big Torski had announced her presence.

Eric was fast, powerful, and focused when he fought, and she'd recognized the dark edge to his moves, the frustration roiling beneath the surface, looking for an outlet. She hadn't seen it at first, but beneath his easy smile and wisecracking was a kindred spirit.

"This place got one of those spar-bots you were telling me about?" she asked.

Eric nodded. "One even Buttercup can use without pulling his punches. Come on, I'll show you." He walked beside her, close enough that his hand brushed hers as they crossed the floor, making her skin tingle pleasantly.

Once they were far enough away, he pitched his voice low and murmured. "It's good to see you again. I wasn't sure they were going to let that happen."

"Your commander insisted I be assessed by an expert on cyborg behavioral conditioning. She reviewed my records and test results, talked to me for a few hours, and determined that I am in my right mind and not being influenced by anyone."

"Was she Pheran? Named Xari or Xori, something like that."

"That's her. Xori Virness. I thought Pheran females were meek, gentle beings. She was...not." The female had been professional, kind, and utterly outraged at the way Nyx had been treated. The dark blue markings on the female's face had darkened to almost black in

82

outrage. The female had written a report then and there, unwilling to leave Nyx alone. "You've been isolated from friends and allies long enough already," she'd said.

Xori had presented a copy of the report to Nyx before leaving to meet with the officers who had deemed her too dangerous to be allowed out of her quarters. As if a few flimsy walls could contain her if she wanted to leave. She'd stayed because she had chosen to, and now she had seen Eric again, she had to admit he was part of the reason she'd chosen not to break out. *But only a small part.*

Eric nodded. "She's treating several other cyborgs who were under corporate control, including the new owner of Astek Corporation. Rossi was smart to bring her in." They reached a squat, multi-limbed machine that sat in the middle of several mats laid out in a rough circle. "This is Bessy."

She nudged the object with her foot. "You named your robot?"

"I didn't. Blink did, the first time Bessy knocked Buttercup on his ass. Her full name is Bessy Beatdown the Badass Battle Bot."

"If I beat her, do I get a cool name, too?"

"If you decide to hang with us, you'll get a nickname eventually. We've all got them. Even Dante's girlfriend." His smile grew wicked and a flash flood of lust rushed through her in a disorienting surge. "I gave her the nickname Daisy."

"For the record, no flower names for me. I've never

even *seen* a flower. Now, how do I turn this thing on? I've been cooped up in my rooms for days and I'd really like to beat up something."

"There is nothing more attractive than a woman who knows what she wants and isn't afraid to say it." He pointed out a large, red button on the bot's upper half. "Tap that. After she's active, you can use basic voice commands. Stop. Defend. Attack. Faster. Slower... harder." His voice dropped to a low rumble on the last word, and she looked up to find him watching her, his dark eyes full of heat.

She hesitated for a moment, wanting to see what he did next. Would he reach for her? Move in closer? Say something that crossed from innuendo to blatant interest? That's what usually happened.

"All you have to do is say the words. You're in control here, Nyx." He tore his gaze from hers to nod toward the bot. "Start her up whenever you're ready."

His words and their multitude of meanings had her head spinning and created an unfamiliar yearning deep in her chest. She'd been alone too much. That was all it was. Even as a prisoner she'd had her connection to her clones to provide her some company, but she hadn't sensed anything like that since she'd been freed. Had her last clone died without her knowing it? Was she really alone in the universe, now?

She activated the bot and fought past her feelings as the machine rose from the floor, all its lights turning green as its various limbs flared out from its core, which now hovered several feet off the ground.

It took her a few minutes to learn how to interact with Bessy, but once she understood the basics, she was able to push herself in ways she'd never been able to before. This wasn't a living being. It wasn't a threat she needed to put down, nor could it feel pain.

She kicked, and hit, and spun, dodging and whirling blows that challenged even her reflexes. It landed enough hits to make her wary, though the damage was minimal. Bruises and scratches her medi-bots could heal in an hour or less. The pain helped her focus, and she reveled in the freedom of pure, straightforward combat.

She held her own for the full round and was still on her feet when Bessy signaled the end of the session with a rapid series of chirps and beeps. The bot's lights all switched to blue, though several indicators strobed amber instead.

"Holy *fraxx*, she broke Bessy," Trinity muttered.

"And they thought they could contain you with a few locked doors and an armed guard?" Dante asked.

"I've never seen anyone move like that. Not even in the matches at the Nova Club."

There were more voices, all familiar, and she looked around to find that the rest of the team had arrived at some point during her workout. She hadn't noticed them, which was noteworthy. She'd never let herself get distracted like that before.

Then she glanced over at Eric and realized she hadn't been distracted. She'd trusted him to watch her back while she fought. That thought struck her harder than any blow the bot had landed. *She trusted him.*

When the hell had that happened? No, scratch that. *Why?* A few shared meals on the ship and some secret conversations didn't mean she could trust him. He couldn't even explain how he had managed to link up to her internal cybernetic channel. All he'd said was it had something to do with reverse hacking Vardarian tech.

Until that conversation, she hadn't even known the Vardarian race existed. She'd read up on them that night. The one thing that being cooped up had given her was plenty of time to catch up on current events. Eric had helped with that, too. He'd been there for her, a constant, steady presence she'd come to enjoy and even rely on. *Dammit, I let him past my guard and didn't even notice.*

"You kicked Bessy's robotic ass. If you ever want to do that professionally, I suspect you'd have no problem getting hired as a cage fighter," Eric said. "Though I'm not sure who they'd find to fight against you."

"That's a profession?" She hadn't considered anything as long term as finding employment. Her only goal was to stay alive and on her feet long enough to take down the man who'd filled her life with misery.

"Cage fighting? Yeah, it's a profession. A high-paying one, in fact. But you don't need to worry about work right now." Dax Rossi joined the conversation. "You're a guest of Nova Force. You don't have to think about making a living yet."

"Guest?" She held up her tracker. "I'm not sure that's the right word. I appreciate what you did to gain me this much freedom, but I'm aware that apart from the people in this room, no one else trusts me, or my motives."

"They'll learn to. These are difficult times, but you just made it very clear that if you'd intended to attack headquarters or harm anyone here, you'd have done it already." Dax looked at the bot, then back to her. "Glad you're on our side, Nyx."

She nodded. She wasn't sure she was on their side, exactly, but they weren't enemies, either.

Eric stayed nearby, waiting until the others had moved on, some working out themselves, others standing around talking. They were a close-knit team who were clearly fond of each other.

"How much freedom are they giving you, exactly?"

"I'm allowed anywhere inside the barracks and common areas. If I want to roam the station, I can, but only with an escort. And it's been mentioned I might want to avoid the Nova Club."

"Yeah, that might be best for now. That's where Echo lived and worked. She had friends there, and what she did…" he sighed and ran a hand through his hair. "Zale was their friend, too. Seeing you will bring all that back for them."

"Like it does for you? You were Echo's lover, after all." And she had some of Echo's memories. Maybe that was why she trusted him. But those experiences belonged to someone else. It was all so damned confusing. When she'd been alone in her cell, it had been easy to keep the memories separate. She had no life experiences of her own. Now, things were muddier. Did she like pizza because she had the memories of other versions of herself liking it, or was that her own choice? Or did they all like pizza because they shared the same neural pathway design?

"I was her lover, yes. But you're not her." The surety in his tone surprised her.

"She was my clone. We're identical."

"Physically, maybe, though you don't have the same mannerisms. You move differently, too. And you are nothing like her in personality. She was sunshine, you're more like starlight."

She decided to be blunt. "And yet you're flirting with me."

He flashed her a wicked little grin. "Yes, I am. You're not Echo, but you're still very much my type."

"Blonde? Athletic?"

He reached for her. His fingertips brushing her cheek before withdrawing again. "Dangerous."

"Right. How could I forget?"

He leaned in a little, dropping his voice to a playful whisper that danced across her senses. "I have no idea. I haven't forgotten a single thing about you since the day we met."

She tried to tell herself it was only flattery, but that didn't stop her heart from racing while her stomach dropped like she'd stepped into zero-g. She should end this flirtation. She didn't need the entanglement, or the distraction. But she liked the way he made her feel. The sense of security. Desirability. It wasn't real, but she could pretend it was, just for a little while. "So, what happens now?"

"Dinner."

That gave her a moment's pause. "What?"

"What happens next is that I take you out to dinner. I think it's time you saw something of Astek station, don't you?"

"I'd like that. Wait, is that allowed? I mean, us - together?"

"Good question." He turned to his commander. "Sir. Given that Nyx is now our guest, is there any reason I couldn't take her out for dinner tonight and show her a bit of the station?"

Aria crowed in triumph. "Ha! Told you so."

Dax stayed silent for several seconds before answering. "I don't see any reason why not. But..."

"Of course there's a but," Eric muttered under his breath.

"But it might be smarter if you weren't the only one in attendance." Dax reached out and took Trinity's hand. "As it happens, Trin and I have no plans for dinner. We can call it a double date."

She was a cyborg assassin, completely immune to emotional reactions like panic, but she had a moment of something damned close to it. She froze, and part of her noted that Eric had done the same.

"Don't torture them, Dax. Or are you forgetting how hard we had to work to sneak away for our first date?" Trinity scolded, her voice light and full of laughter.

"Which first date?" Dax grinned and tugged his wife to his side so he could kiss her cheek.

"Both."

"Good point." Dax looked up, still grinning. "Let us know the time and place, and we'll walk over with you, but I promise we'll have separate tables." He gave them an understanding look. "This protects both of you. I know it's not ideal, but no one is going to complain if Trin and I are there, too."

"I get it. I even appreciate what you're doing. That doesn't mean I like that it's necessary," Eric said.

Nyx interjected. "I don't understand. I was told I could roam the station so long as I had a Nova Force member with me. Why do I need three of you to have dinner somewhere?" Now she was over her shock – she still wasn't calling it panic – she was struggling to understand.

Eric grunted. "Dax and Trin aren't there for you, starshine. They'll be keeping tabs on me."

"You? Why?"

Dante spoke. "Our benevolent overlords think Magi's dangerous, too."

"Of course he is, he's one of us. We're Nova Force. We're supposed to be dangerous," Aria said with pride.

"Is that so?" she asked.

Eric nodded, a hint of defiant pride in his gaze. "It is. I'll tell you about it tonight. That is, if you're still interested."

She was more than interested. She was intrigued. "Just tell me when."

"I'll send someone over with the exact time once I've made reservations at a place I know. Good food. Nice music. I think you'll like it."

"I trust you."

He beamed. "I'm honored. I promise, you'll have fun tonight."

"Okay." She had no idea what fun was. Not really. But she was looking forward to finding out. And while they were enjoying themselves, she'd find out what she could about the investigation and why Eric's own people didn't completely trust him. It should be an interesting night.

CHAPTER SEVEN

NYX FINISHED OFF HER WORKOUT, then returned to her rooms to shower. She'd already memorized the basic layout of Nova Force's headquarters. There was an administration area, barracks, and a basic med-center. There were also common areas for meeting, exercise, and dining for those who wanted company while they ate.

The space was shared with the IAF. She'd learned enough about the Gray Men and the general instability of the Drift to know that the Intergalactic Armed Forces had moved a large number of soldiers into the area in an attempt to restore order to what had become a hotspot for intrigue and violence between the corporations. She'd seen dozens of soldiers and support staff since arriving on the station, but only a handful of civilians. Most of those had been doctors and technicians who were brought in to assess her implants and her health - both physical and mental.

Out of everyone she'd interacted with, the civilians had been the nicest. She'd been prepared to be treated like a test subject again, but it hadn't been that way at all. There'd been no pain or degradation. Everyone had explained what they were doing, and why it was being done. One of them had even recommended several dishes from the food dispenser, including a savory steamed dumpling called *jiaozi.* They'd proven to be delicious, and she'd had them several times since. Now that she had more freedom, she really needed to find a way to thank Dr. Li for the recommendation.

Eric's messenger didn't take long to arrive. An hour after she'd left the gym, her door chimed, announcing she had a visitor.

"Who is it?" she called as she rose from her monitor. Eric had given her a list of books, vids, and articles he recommended, and she'd been working her way through them as a means of passing the time between tests and interrogations.

"I come bearing messages, and gifts." A woman's voice announced through the closed door. It was familiar, and it only took a second for Nyx to connect the voice pattern to a name.

"Dr. Li?" she opened the door, a simple act that declared her freedom every time she did it. Dr. Li was of less than average height, with dark hair touched with a few strands of silver and a warm, friendly smile.

"Hello, again. Eric asked me to come by. Your dinner is at eighteen-hundred hours tonight. He'll be by to pick you up fifteen minutes before." The woman raised her arms, indicating the two large bags she carried. "And I thought I might be able to help you find something to wear."

"You know Eric? I mean, clearly you do, but I didn't realize, and Eric didn't say anything." She stepped aside and gestured. "Come in."

"Eric didn't know I was one of the doctors brought in to assess you. Security protocols and all that. Trinity knew, though, and she updated him a little while ago. Oh, and please, call me Tyra. I'm not here in any official capacity."

"And you're willing to play messenger? I thought he'd send over one of the soldiers who've been escorting me around the base."

Tyra beamed and waved a golden-skinned hand. "It was no trouble. Dante and I are in the family quarters just down that way."

"You're Daisy! I didn't realize."

Tyra nodded. "I couldn't tell you before, protocol again. But now you've been cleared, I wanted to come by and say hello." She set down the bags. "I'm so glad they found you."

"Me, too." The silence stretched out after that as she struggled to come up with something else to say. Social niceties were not something she had much practice with, but she wanted to acknowledge Tyra's kindness. "Oh! I meant to thank you for the dumpling recommendation. They really are delicious. I've had them for several meals."

"Delicious and high calorie. Which is exactly what you need. I'm glad you liked them."

"I did." Silence fell again.

This time, it was Tyra who broke it. She opened her arms and moved closer. "I'd like to hug you. Would that be okay?"

"Hug me? Why?"

"Because I think you could use one."

She nodded, and a second later Tyra had her arms wrapped around her in a gentle hug. The other woman didn't quite reach her shoulder, so Nyx ended up draping her arms awkwardly over Tyra's shoulders to hug her back. It was nice. Warm and gentle, and she uttered a small sigh that left her feeling more relaxed.

"I was right. You needed a hug." Tyra gave her a final squeeze, then stepped back. "I know what it's like to be out of your element and dependant on strangers."

"You do? But you're a doctor. You've got Dante and…" She raised her hands, trying to encompass the size of the world Tyra lived in. "All this."

"And when I met Dante the first time, I was running for my life, scared, hungry, and alone. Hiding from the bastards who killed my medical team. If it weren't for Nico and his friends taking me in, if Dante hadn't found us, my story would have ended quite differently."

"Nico? So, he's not your child, or Dante's?"

"He's ours in every way that matters."

"Then he's a lucky boy."

"I think I'm the lucky one." Tyra smiled, the expression crinkling her eyes at the corners. "And that's enough about me. This visit is supposed to be about you. Would you like to try these on alone, or would you rather have some company?"

She'd had enough of being alone. "Stay, please."

"I'm happy to." Tyra gestured to the bags. "Point me to the bedroom and we'll start trying these on. They're custom tailored, but some of them will still look better than others."

"Custom? How?"

Tyra gave her a mischievous look, her dark eyes sparkling. "How many medical scans have you undergone in the last week? I might have liberated the data on your measurements, for a good cause, of course. And, I was told you are now considered a guest here, which means you're on Nova Force's expense account."

Nyx stared at the woman, then the bags. Part of her was itching to empty them out and see what Tyra had bought, but she had misgivings. If she kept letting people into her life, things would get messy.

Things are already messy. Come on, think it through. You've agreed to go out for dinner. If you don't do this with Tyra, what are you going to wear tonight? More workout gear?

"So? Bedroom?" Tyra glanced around, then frowned. "Wait a second. There's only one door, and I'm guessing from the steam lingering around it that's where your shower is. So, where do you sleep?"

Instead of answering, Nyx stepped to an open stretch of wall and touched a switch set into it. Part of the floor rolled back, and a neatly-made single bed rose from the floor, locking into position at right angles to the wall. "It's a multi-functional space. At least, that's how Trinity explained it to me when she gave me the tour." She shrugged. "It was a very short tour."

"They've had you cooped up in here all this time? ~~Someone needs to remind~~ Colonel Bahl and Archer that we're supposed to be the good guys. This isn't much better than a prison cell." Tyra stopped mid-rant, her eyes wide. "Sorry. That was a poor choice of words. But this? This isn't right."

"It's fine. And honestly, it's a lot nicer than the last three cells I had. There's food, and blankets, and a soft place to sleep. I'm in control of the temperature, the lights. And I've got books to read. Vids to watch."

Tyra huffed. "It still sucks harder than a black hole. And the décor is…ugh. Why does the military think that everything needs to be painted gray?"

Nyx looked around. The doctor was right. Everything around her was gray or white. The walls, the floors, even the blankets on her bed.

Tyra grabbed one of the bags and upended it, spilling the contents onto the bed in a rainbow.

There were tops, pants, dresses, and skirts in a variety of cuts, colors, and fabrics. Words attached themselves to some of the cloth, programmed information she'd never needed to access until now. There was a dress of red *Keski* silk and a top made from velvet so soft her fingers left marks as she moved her hand over it. "Where do I even start?"

"We start with a mirror. Then, I think you should try

this one on." Tyra handed her a dress from the pile. It was a shimmering blue-green color, and the fabric was so soft it flowed through her fingers like cool water.

"Computer, reflective surface, main wall." The flat gray surface rippled from top to bottom, transforming into a mirror that took up most of the wall.

"Basic AI interface? Nice to know they gave you that much." Tyra took a seat and gestured. "So, put it on. I think that one's going to knock Eric out of orbit."

"It's just dinner."

Tyra laughed. "That's what I said, too. And now I'm living with him."

A pang of envy, sharp and hot, sliced through her. Tyra had a good life, with love, laughter, and friends. Nyx couldn't see a future like that. Not for her. She wasn't even sure she deserved a life like Tyra's. None of her clones had gotten that chance. She was a killer with a limited skill set, and she only planned on putting those skills to use one more time. Once Absalom was dead, she wouldn't need to do anything else.

"I'm not sure that's in the cards for me." She stripped out of the simple t-shirt and shorts she'd been wearing and slipped the dress over her head, letting the cool fabric slide over her skin like a caress.

"Life's funny. It can sneak up on you while you're busy making other plans." There was a pause, then, "Oh, wow. That dress is stunning on you."

She looked at the mirror and made a tiny sound of shock as she saw her reflection and barely recognized the woman standing there. The dress was styled perfectly, molding to her newly acquired curves without feeling restrictive or uncomfortable, and the color was beautiful, like the pictures she'd seen of oceans.

For the first time in her life, she felt beautiful. It had never mattered before. As a soldier and test subject, she didn't think about her appearance. What would be the point? She'd been forged as a weapon and used as a tool, but she was more than that now. She was a woman as well as a warrior, beautiful as well as strong.

She ran a hand over the dress, smoothing the fabric over her midriff. "I hardly recognize myself right now. I'm definitely going to wear this tonight." She looked over the rest of the garments. "I guess the rest can go back. I don't need to try on anything else."

Tyra shook her head. "Nope. These are all yours, bought and paid for. Commander Rossi approved the purchase already." She gestured to the stack, then to the other bag, still sitting on the floor. "That bag has an assortment of shoes, a killer pair of boots, and non-regulation underwear. IAF standard-issue undies won't work with that dress. Practical has its place, but sometimes, a girl has got to go with satin and lace."

"If you say so." She'd never worn underwear until recently.

"Try a pair on. You'll see." Tyra rose to her feet. "In fact, you do that now, and I'm going to go find us both something to drink. Please tell me they've loaded your food dispenser with a decent wine selection, or I'm going to have to call Dante for a delivery."

"I don't know how good it is, but there's wine."

"Perfect. I'll be right back."

Nyx carefully undressed and took a moment to hang the dress in her almost empty closet. Then she grabbed the other bag and emptied it onto the bed, forming a second pile of shoes and scraps of fabric that were more lace than substance.

"These aren't garments, they're frothy bits of nothing."

"Exactly. Extremely impractical, and designed to make any male lose his mind the moment he sees them." Tyra called from the far side of the room.

"Eric is not seeing these. It's just dinner."

"This is your first date, right?" Tyra asked.

"Right." She had memories of going out with Eric, but they belonged to Echo. The furies had seduced men and even a few women, and she had parts of those recollections, too. They weren't hers, though. She wasn't living vicariously anymore. Tonight, she'd make her own memories, while there was still time.

"Then trust me when I tell you that if you wear that dress tonight, Eric will be putty in those cybernetically enhanced hands of yours."

"He will?"

Tyra crossed back to her and handed her a glass of white wine. "Absolutely. Drink up. You've got more outfits to try on."

ERIC HAD WORK TO DO, but he couldn't concentrate for more than a few minutes at a time. The data he was working on was badly fragmented and needed his full attention, but today that just wasn't going to happen. The sense of familiarity had struck him again while he was working, a pattern of code he'd seen before, but he hadn't rebuilt enough of it to be recognizable. His instincts told him that this was a big piece of the puzzle, one he'd need to get exactly right if they were going to figure out what Absalom was up to and where he might have gone next.

He withdrew from cyberspace faster than he should have, and it took him a few seconds to gather his wits and re-oriented himself in reality. Spend too much time jacked in, and you started to forget about reality, which was a problem, because that's where your body was, and a body wouldn't last long without basics like food and water.

He was working from his quarters, which wasn't unusual if he was going to be jacked-in. It minimized interruptions, and prevented his teammates from messing with his body while his mind was elsewhere. They'd done everything from tying him to his chair to using elaborate props to stage holo-pics that had taken him weeks to scrub from existence.

A quick check of the time told him he had about an hour before his date with Nyx. By now, Tyra should have stopped by to deliver his message and he wanted to know what she'd brought for Nyx to wear. He had a few minutes to check in with her before he needed to get ready. He reached down and pressed his thumb to a scanner embedded into the underside of his desk. A moment later, a panel slid open, revealing a small stash of devices and tech that he'd prefer his employers never learn he had. He picked up what looked like a simple earpiece with a data jack, settled it into place, then inserted the jack into the port behind his ear.

It was a prototype he was working on, a combination of Vardarian and human tech that he hoped would one day allow humans to utilize the same cybernetic channels the cyborgs used to communicate with each other. It was still a work in progress, though. He'd designed the one he used to work with his own existing modifications, but for it to work with others, they'd have to have the devices permanently implanted. Before he got to that step, he'd need to bring in medical and cybernetic experts, and he had a lot of work to do before that happened.

Work that could wait. Right now, he wanted to talk to Nyx. *"Hi. You free to talk?"*

"I am. I'm readying myself for our date tonight. Some of the shoes Tyra brought are lovely, but not easy to walk in. I am deciding if I wish to limit my combat-readiness for the sake of fashion."

He grinned and wished he could see her expression. *"Wear what makes you feel comfortable, though I can almost guarantee you're not going to need to fight anyone tonight. This is dinner and maybe dancing, but there's no bloodshed on the agenda."*

"Dancing? You didn't mention that before. I don't dance."

"That's good, because I don't really know how, either. I'm more of a stand and sway to the music sort of dancer."

"I could manage that, but not in these shoes. I will wear one of the other pairs."

"Sensible. But I'm sorry I won't get to see you in the impractical shoes. I bet they look great."

"You wish to see my shoes?" she sounded perplexed.

"I want to see you. All of you. Shoes. Dress. The works. In case no one's warned you, I'm not good at waiting."

"You've seen me before. Well, you've seen Echo. We are similar enough."

"But not the same. I know the difference." In fact, the differences were becoming clearer to him all the time.

"If you truly wish to see me..." she paused for a few seconds before continuing. *"There."*

His comms chimed softly, announcing he had an incoming message. It was a single file, and he opened it eagerly. It was an image of Nyx wearing a dress that flowed over her curves, showing just enough skin to be tantalizing. She was standing in front of a full-length mirror, posed so that the slit in her dress showed off her shapely leg and the sparkling bits of silver strapping that somehow wove together to form footwear. *"Wow. You look incredible. I'm going to be fighting off half the station when they get a look at you."*

"You said there would be no fighting." It was hard to be sure, but he thought he detected a teasing note to her words.

"I hadn't seen you in that dress when I said that."

"If that happens, you won't be fighting alone."

"I'd be honored to have you at my side no matter what the circumstances." He winced at how formal and stilted that sounded, but he didn't want to say more. Not yet. He knew what he wanted from her, and it was a lot more than just having her at his side. Now that he was allowed to see her again, he was going to do all he could to make that happen.

Then, a thought occurred. "How did you send me that file?"

This time there was no mistaking the laughter in her voice. "I was wondering how long it would take you to ask that question. Tyra brought me a comm unit. It had contact information for you, her, and the rest of the team."

"So, we could have had this conversation by comms? With vid-screens?"

"We could have. But then I wouldn't have you in my head."

He grinned. "And you like me there?"

"I do. Besides, they'll be monitoring all my communications. This is still the only way we can speak freely. I need to know what's happening with the investigation, and now that your leaders have decided to trust me, I want you to tell me all of it."

"I will, but I have questions for you, too. You haven't told them everything, have you?"

"What makes you say that?" Nyx asked with the barest of hesitations.

"Because so far, everyone is talking about your clones in

the past tense. Only they're not all gone, are they?" He'd caught her slip that first day, when she'd mentioned other furies. She'd said they *are* special and quickly corrected herself. He wasn't the most experienced interrogator on the team, but he was learning quickly, and that had been an important moment.

"I don't know."

"You haven't sensed them?"

"No."

And that confirmed it for him. She hadn't denied there was anyone left. She'd only admitted she hadn't sensed them, which meant at least one of her clones was still alive, or had been last she knew. *"We'll talk. There are things I need to tell you."*

"I want to know why your leaders don't trust you."

"I know. But surely you've guessed at least some of it by now."

Again, her words were accompanied by a delicate note of amusement. *"We'll talk. But now, you need to get ready, or you're going to be late for our date."*

He glanced at the time and realized she was right. *"I'll see you soon, starshine."*

"I'm looking forward to it."

"So am I." He was finally getting a chance to be alone with Nyx. Tomorrow he'd go back to work. Tonight, he was going to enjoy himself.

CHAPTER EIGHT

THEIR DESTINATION WAS a short walk down the main concourse of Astek station, and Nyx drank in every second of the journey. It was a noisy, crowded place, full of beings from across the galaxy. Massive Torskis, Jeskyran's, their yellow skin erupting in clusters of thorns, blue-haired Pherans, and humans of every shape and size.

"Is it always like this?" she asked as they passed a group of clearly intoxicated humans singing something both bawdy and horribly off-key.

"Pretty much. Astek is a pleasure station, a place for the miners and freighter crews to blow off steam and spend their hard-earned scrip on a bit of fun and company before they head out again. Most of these beings are here for a few days at most." Eric made an expansive gesture that included the crowd, the vendors, and the various entertainment venues that advertised with loud music and dazzling holographic displays. "Welcome to the Drift, Nyx."

"And you live here, in the middle of all this chaos?"

He grinned. "Isn't it great? Our last base wasn't nearly this entertaining."

Dax snorted from his place just ahead of them. "Entertaining? I'm with Nyx on this one. This is chaos." He turned to look back at them. "But the spot we're going is quite something. Nothing like it in the Ibex system."

"Ibex is the home system for the IAF, right?"

"It is, though there's scuttlebutt that they might be sending a portion of the fleet out this way," Eric said.

"I've seen seventeen IAF uniforms since we entered the public areas. Based on that, I'd say the IAF is already here."

Eric gave her a sidelong look and a grin. "Seventeen, huh? Someone's operating at high alert. I thought we agreed there'd be no bloodshed tonight."

"You said there was almost no chance of fighting. That's not the same thing." She gave him an appraising glance. He wore a black shirt with subtle threads of red running through the fabric, black pants that fitted his muscular form with undeniable style, and a belt that included a holstered blaster. "And I might be aware of my surroundings, but I'm not armed, which is more than can be said for the three of you."

Trinity turned and smiled. "From what I've seen, you don't need to be armed to be dangerous. It's a precaution, nothing more. Your captors lost a valuable asset when you were freed. We want to be sure that no one tries to take you back."

"You're protecting me?" The idea that anyone would do that was so foreign to her she stopped walking to process it.

Eric turned to face her, his expression fierce. "Damn right we are. No one is taking your freedom again, Nyx. Nova Force was created to stop the corporations from breaking galactic law. We failed to protect you once, that's not going to happen again."

"I can take care of myself."

He reached down and took her hand, his gaze never leaving her face. "I know. But you don't have to do it alone."

An unfamiliar flare of heat rushed up her cheeks, and she had to force her next words past an odd tightening in her throat. "Thank you."

He threaded his fingers through hers and squeezed her hand. "I mean it. You're not on your own anymore. You have me. You have us."

She surprised them both by leaning in to kiss the corner of his mouth. "Thank—"

He turned his head and captured her lips with his, cutting off her whispered words of thanks. His free hand slipped around her waist, drawing her against him as his lips slanted across hers. His mouth seared hers in a hard, hot kiss that ended far too quickly. He released her and stepped back, keeping her hand in his.

"Dinner?" he asked, his blithe tone belying the heat that still lingered in his eyes.

"Um. What? Oh, yes. Dinner. Dinner would be good." She shook her head in an attempt to clear her muddled thoughts. She was an assassin, created to kill anyone at any time. One kiss, no matter how good it was, should not render her incapable of answering a simple *fraxxing* question.

They walked the rest of the way in silence. Dax and Trinity stayed just in front of them, their hands linked in the same way as hers and Eric's. Their destination proved to be a place called Amped, which had a lineup of beings waiting to get in. She assumed they'd be joining the queue, but Eric led her straight to the doors and spoke with one of the security guards. He checked a datapad, nodded, and gestured for them to go inside.

"No line?" she asked.

"I know the owners. They were happy to reserve two tables for tonight. Ours is over there," he pointed to a slightly raised area somewhat secluded from the rest of the space. "And Dax and Trinity will be dining over there." He pointed to an empty table tucked into a cozy corner on the far side of the room.

"Subtle, Magi," Dax commented drily.

"But romantic," Trinity added. "Come on. We haven't been out on a date since we got married. It's like you're not even trying anymore."

"I don't need to try. You said yes, I won. Game over."

"Game over?" Trinity cocked her head and placed a hand on her hip. "Commander Rossi, you take that back, or you can sleep on the ship tonight!"

Dax gave his wife a wicked smile. "Who said anything about sleeping tonight?"

Trinity blushed. "Behave."

"Only when we're on duty, Butterfly."

It was a beautiful, intimate peek into Dax and Trin's relationship, and Nyx felt both envy and admiration for the pair. They clearly loved each other, but she'd spent enough time with them to know they were both strong personalities. Finding a balance couldn't have been easy, but seeing the way they were together… That was something worth fighting for.

Eric groaned in mock horror and made a shooing gesture. "Ugh, isn't there a rule that married people are not supposed to flirt with each other? If you have to do that, go do it at your table - way over there."

They parted company then, and Eric led her to their seats. The club was laid out with plenty of space between the tables, giving the servers ample room to move and allowing the patrons at least the illusion of privacy as they dined. The furniture all looked comfortable and stylish, with high backs and thick cushions done in dark reds and shades of gold. The dark paneling on the walls was almost hidden by all the photos hung on it, and she adjusted her vision for the low light, zooming in enough to make out that most of the images were of musicians, playing or posing with their instruments.

They had to pass another security guard to reach their table. "Is the guard here to protect me, too?" She asked, amused.

"Him? No. This is a private area. No one without a reservation is allowed in here. It's his job to keep out the riff-raff." Eric held out a chair for her, an archaic but oddly pleasing gesture.

Once they were both seated, she asked, "How exactly did you manage to arrange all this at the last minute? I know you said you knew the owners, but this is a pretty big favor."

"I helped T'arv set up the AI that runs the lights and sound equipment. While I was inside the system, I might have noticed that there are actually four owners, not two. T'arv and his wife run this place, but there are two cyborgs who act as silent partners." Eric chuckled. "They know I know. And occasionally I ask them for a favor, like oh, a table in the VIP section."

"That's blackmail!"

"Not really. They're friends, and they work at Corp-Sec. I do them favors when I can, too."

She arched a brow. "Favors that might get you in trouble if you were caught?"

"Sometimes." He admitted. He shrugged one shoulder, looking utterly unrepentant. "My friends trust me because they know I'd do anything to help them. Anything, Nyx."

"Which is the same reason the IAF brass don't trust you, right?"

"One of the reasons." He touched the light cube that illuminated their table, re-setting it to a softer, golden glow. "Before we get into that, I want to hear about your day. Did Tyra stay and visit for a bit today? I wasn't sure if you'd want her to, given how you two first met and all."

"She stayed. We had wine and I tried on more clothes than I've worn in my entire life. It was enjoyable. And I like Tyra. Thank you for asking her to visit me. She was kind."

"She's a good person, and a friend. I hate that I didn't know she was part of your assessment. Secrets aren't a good thing, especially not when they involve my friends, or my team."

A server approached the table, and they paused in the conversation to order. She let Eric choose, he knew her tastes better than anyone else in the galaxy.

Once they were alone again, he reached across the table and waited until she placed her hand in his. "That's better. I've missed talking to you like this."

"I don't ever remember talking like this," she squeezed his fingers. "This is new. Like that kiss."

"I'm hoping you let me kiss you again before this night is over."

"I don't remember *letting* you kiss me last time. It just happened."

He stroked his thumb across her skin. "Well, you didn't throw me through a wall, so I took that as a good sign."

"I didn't throw you through a wall because you're my friend. I don't know much about friendship, but I'm pretty sure you don't do that to people you… care about." She almost didn't say the last two words, but something made her do it.

"I care about you, too." He stood and walked around their table to stand beside her, then tugged at her hand until she rose to her feet. Without a word, he stepped into the shadows that shrouded the back wall of the space and pulled her into his arms.

"What are we doing?"

"Something that's undoubtedly going to get me in trouble."

Laughter bubbled up inside her and she let it spill out as she slipped her arms around his waist. "I'm starting to notice a pattern. Where you go, trouble follows."

He cupped her cheek in one hand, stroking his thumb over her lower lip and smiling at her. "And yet you're still here."

"Why wouldn't I be?"

He chuckled and pressed a kiss to the tip of her nose. "Because most women don't like trouble, not for more than a night or two."

"From what I've seen, life is full of trouble whether you want it or not. I think I'd rather be with someone who actually knows how to deal with trouble when it comes." She paused, then hastily added, "Not that I'm with you. I don't know what we are, exactly, or how long we've got to be…whatever this is."

"I'm not sure what this is, either. Not yet." He kissed her then, slow and sweet. His mouth moved over hers, tasting and teasing, and she leaned into him, kissing him back for the first time. He whispered her name in a low, husky tone that sent a delicious shiver running down her spine.

Heat pooled low in her belly and she gave into the needs flowing through her, pressing herself against the hard lines of his body and running her hands up his body. Flanks, chest, shoulders, and finally letting her fingers brush over the scars on his neck and up into his dark, curling hair.

He groaned, his tongue tracing the seam of her lips with a questing hunger that made her body throb. She opened her mouth to him, a low moan of need escaping her throat as the kiss deepened, and her senses reeled from the pure, boundless pleasure of it all.

His hands were strong, steady, and sure as they caressed her, his desire for her flatteringly obvious from the hard line of his cock pressed against her stomach to the way his heart raced and his body temperature spiked the moment their mouths touched. She registered it all, memorizing every detail.

They stayed that way, entwined and breathless, until she sensed a presence on the stairs. Their server was returning with their drinks. Eric noticed, too, ending their kiss but keeping her cradled to his side, one arm still wrapped around her waist.

The server was discreet, setting out their glasses with only a slight nod in their direction. "Dinner will be arriving soon," was all she said as she left.

Eric chuckled and she could feel the vibration of his laughter deep in his chest. "In other words, we should get back to our table before they serve our meal to a couple of empty chairs."

"Which would be a waste of good food. Is ravioli as enjoyable to eat as it is to say?"

"Better. Nadia is an amazing chef, and she recommended I order that today when I made the reservation."

"And they really don't mind that we took this whole section? They could have other paying customers in here if it weren't for your request." It didn't feel right to her that their presence might have cost Eric's friends fairly earned income. She'd already learned enough about the station to know that living here was expensive. Everything they consumed had to be imported great distances, and resources like air, water, and real estate were all finite and had to be carefully managed.

He kissed her lightly. "Don't worry. I made sure they were compensated fairly."

"So, you blackmailed them into giving us a private table, then gave them scrip to cover the difference?"

His lips quirked and he looked a little sheepish. "Yeah."

She touched her hand to his chest and snuggled into his side, feeling a warm sense of contentment and security as she looked into his eyes. "You've got a soft heart. I never understood that expression until now."

Eric didn't answer her with words, but his next kiss spoke volumes. It was passionate and at the same time tender, and she'd remember this kiss for the rest of her life. She'd keep her promises and end the ones who had hurt her, but until then, she was going to steal a few moments of happiness and create some memories of her own.

DINNER ARRIVED SHORTLY after they returned to their seats. It was the promised ravioli, along with freshly baked bread slathered in butter and a side of synthesized vegetable matter roasted to golden perfection. Eric barely looked at it. He wanted to ignore it all, pull Nyx onto his lap, and kiss her until T'arv threw them out.

Instead, he casually withdrew a small device from his pocket and set it on the table by the light cube, tapping it twice. The noise level around them dropped significantly.

"Portable sound dampener. I thought it would make it easier to talk."

She gave him a knowing smile that made him think about kissing her again. "While making sure we're not overheard?"

"Exactly."

She ate a few more bites, then asked him the same question she'd asked earlier. "Why don't they trust you?"

He took a sip of wine. "Because before I worked for Nova Force, I worked against them."

Her fork hovered mid-way between her plate and her lips. "What?"

He pointed to the data-port behind his ear. "I was a hacker. Part of a loosely affiliated group of cyber-jockeys who were trying to make a difference. At least, that's what we thought we were doing. We stole secrets and outed them to the public. Corporations, governments, the IAF. It didn't matter who they were."

"You got caught."

He nodded. "I got caught, but I wasn't alone. Hacking was a family business. I learned it from my dad. What I did with him wasn't as noble, but it made sure we lived well and could afford the best implants on the black market."

"Your mother allowed this to happen?"

Eric snorted. "It was the *family* business, Nyx. She knew what my father was when she married him. She was an engineer on Hadfield station, where I grew up. Hadfield wasn't much different from this one - older, worn down, and in constant need of repairs. Some of the money dad made got channeled into Mom's repair budget. She would have liked me to become an engineer like her, but…" He shrugged.

"But honest work didn't pay nearly as well?"

He watched her expression, looking for judgment or condemnation, and found neither. "Not nearly as well. And I thought I could make a difference."

"Did you?" she asked.

The question surprised him. No one had asked him that before. He thought about it a moment. "I think I did. But it came at too high a price. Especially the bit where my dad and I wound up facing prison sentences."

She cocked her head thoughtfully. "They offered you a deal, didn't they?"

"They did. Colonel Divya Bahl paid me a visit the day before our trial. If I joined the IAF and made it through basic training I'd be transferred to Nova Force and put to work. I'd get probation, but more importantly, if I held up my end of the deal, they'd arrange for my dad to get a reduced sentence and transfer him to a prison colony on a farming planet. No cells. No guards." At the time, he'd agreed because he'd had no choice. Now, he was grateful for the offer. It had changed his life. These days he really was helping to make a difference in the galaxy.

"Do you get to see him?"

"Sometimes. I've arranged for a couple of visits over the years. Mom went with him. They actually like it there. They get to use their skills to help the community, fresh air, honest work. Dad's served his time, now, but they stayed on."

"Then it all worked out. Mostly."

"Mostly," he agreed. "But some of the things I did back then had unexpected consequences. Big ones."

"Like what?"

"I stole data that proved a major shipping company was using recycled hardware in their systems to cut costs. The systems were unstable and plagued by malfunctions. One ship nav system failed and the crew died when their course took them straight into a star. Another ship suffered a total life support malfunction."

Guilt stirred in his gut, and he washed some of the bitter taste from his mouth with another drink of wine.

"I got hold of the data proving they were responsible for the deaths, and Bardeaux's stock took a major hit. They had to close some of their shipyards. Because of me, several thousand people on the factory worlds that supplied those yards lost their jobs and their homes. On top of that, Bardeaux was the chief rival of Bellex Corp. What I did set them back a few years, and gave Bellex a chance to increase their profit margin. Bellex used that money to engage in some seriously *fraxxed* up, illegal crap that my team had to clean on a recent mission."

"But you got the chance to balance the scales?"

"Yeah, I did."

She set down her fork and reached across the table, touching the back of his hand. "Then you're luckier than most. I'll never be able to undo the deaths I'm responsible for. All I can do is ensure Absalom and his people won't do it again."

"You've been a prisoner your whole life. What deaths could you be responsible for? I mean, besides the guards you took down when escaping."

Her gray eyes grew stormy. "Every life my clones took. In every way that mattered, every fury to ever draw breath was *me*. If I'd found a way to escape. If I'd stopped them sooner..." she took a ragged breath, her voice heavy with regrets. "And the furies, too. Their suffering is my fault. I was created to kill, Eric, and that meant they were, too. When Absalom realized that he could help fund his nightmare endeavors by selling some of the furies into service as assassins, he didn't hesitate. They're almost all gone now, and I witnessed every one of their deaths."

"You were a prisoner, Nyx. None of what happened was your fault. It was that bastard Absalom. I wish I could introduce you to some of the other clones I know. None of them would ever consider themselves the same person. Hell, Vic and Ward were used as assassins, too. The corporation treated them like interchangeable parts, but they're two separate entities. *Veth*, I wish you could talk to them."

"But I can't, because Echo killed someone they cared about, and when they see me, they're going to see her, instead," Nyx stated flatly, as if that fact somehow proved her point.

"But you're not her." He captured her hand in his. "It's bad enough you have to carry the memory of their deaths, you are not responsible for what they did while they were alive."

"I think I do." She tensed, and for a moment he thought she was going to pull away from him. Instead, she exhaled sharply and closed her eyes. "I'm sorry. This isn't something I want to talk about tonight."

"Alright. We'll table that topic for now. Someday though, we're going to talk about it again."

She opened her eyes and gave him a small smile. "Brave man, trying to tell me what to do."

"Did it work?" He flashed her a playful smile and squeezed her hand. He'd tease her until she threatened to break him in half if it meant he didn't have to see her hurting.

"What do you think?" Her smile brightened.

"I think we're going to need more wine. Then you're going to tell me about the fury that's still alive. After that, you get to ask me all the questions you like, about anything. If I can tell you, I will."

"Anything? You're right. We're going to need more wine."

The night's performers came out on stage a few minutes later, and Eric adjusted the sound dampener so they could enjoy the music. They finished their meals and listened to the band until they ended their first set. Two chocolate sundaes arrived for dessert, along with a fresh carafe of wine, and once they were alone again, Nyx turned up the dampening field again.

"You want to know about the last fury," she said without preamble.

"I do."

"You were right. There's one still alive out there. At least, I think she is. I haven't sensed anything from her since a few days before you found me."

"Nothing? Is that normal?"

"No. Not with her. My connection to my clones varies. I'm not sure why. I think it has something to do with the adjustments they make to their individual design matrixes. Some of them were barely more than a flicker in my awareness. Most of them, I got occasional flashes, usually when they were in pain or highly emotional. There were a few where the connection was strong enough we could sense each other." She smiled, but her eyes were sad. "They were my only company, and from the moment I became aware of them, I knew they were destined to die."

"Like Echo. That's how she knew about you." And if they'd sensed each other, Echo must have known how much Nyx suffered. No wonder she'd fought her conditioning to get a message to him, asking him to find Nyx.

"Exactly. My link to this last clone is strong, but I haven't felt her presence at all. I think, maybe, they've put her in cryo. They do that when they're moving us around. We're much more manageable as cargo than as prisoners."

"If you sensed her again, could you find her?"

She stiffened slightly, a minute change in posture he would have missed if Aria hadn't been teaching him to read body language. She was considering lying to him.

"I don't know. Maybe? She'd have to be able to tell me where she was. This connection doesn't act like a homing signal. It's just…there."

He exhaled deeply. It wasn't the news he'd been hoping for, but she hadn't lied to him. "Who was she working with the last time you had contact?"

"If I tell you, are you going to tell your team?"

"Do you want me to?"

They stared at each other for several painfully long

moments. This was uncharted space for both of them. "For now? No."

"Okay. For now, I won't." At the moment, he didn't have hard intel to give to anyone, anyway.

"She was with Absalom. I think he's using her as part of his personal security team."

"Isn't that risky? I mean, he knows that the furies eventually become self-aware, right?

"He has ways of controlling us. There'd be some risk, but not much."

"And you think she's with him now. So if you sense her again, you might be able to find her, and Absalom, too?"

"Maybe." She raised her hands. "I can't make any promises."

"Then for now, there's no reason to tell anyone, is there? It's all hypothetical."

"Yes, it is." She relaxed a little and started eating her dessert again.

Once she was done, she pushed the dish aside and leaned in. "So, my turn now?"

"Your turn." He'd been expecting her to ask about the mission to find Absalom, or his life before Nova Force. He owed her the truth, no matter what question she asked.

"Do you want to kiss me again?"

His mouth opened, but for a second no words came out because his brain was completely distracted by the victory dance he was doing in his head. "Hell, yes, I want to kiss you again."

"Then we're done talking for now." She rose. "Turn off that dampener and dance with me. Kiss me. Show me what I've been missing all these years."

He moved faster than if they were in a firefight. In seconds he had the device back in his pocket and Nyx in his arms. He pulled her in close as he turned her, moving her into the shadows at the back of the room. The music flowed around them, a slow, romantic ballad he hadn't even noticed, though he suspected she had.

He was on fire for her, wanted to peel her out of her dress and devour every inch of her beautiful body. She was a collection of contrasts that intrigued him. Steel wrapped in silk. A jaded innocent. An assassin with a gentle soul. She was all of that, and more.

He held her close, letting her feel the way her body affected his. He was hard and aching for her, and she rubbed herself against him with a sensual grace that had him fighting back a groan of raw need.

He claimed her mouth, kissing her deeply, drinking in the sweet taste of her lips, the sticky delight of chocolate sauce and whipped cream. Their tongues tangled, and he finally loosed the groan he'd been holding back. She uttered a soft moan in return, her hands hotter than flames, almost searing him through his shirt as she caressed his chest and shoulders.

Their dance didn't end with the music. They stayed where they were, swaying in time to the beat of their hearts until he was drunk with desire. "Come home with me tonight, Nyx."

She lifted her hand, showing him the tracker on her wrist. "If I do that, they'll know about us."

"I don't care. They already think I'm emotionally compromised when it comes to you, starshine. We might as well make it official."

"Are you?" Her gray eyes were bright as molten silver as she looked at him.

"Emotionally compromised?" He pressed his forehead to hers to look her in the eyes. "Absolutely."

She uttered a delightful little laugh he'd never heard from her before. "I think I might be, too."

CHAPTER NINE

THE WALK back took far longer than it should have because Eric kept stopping to kiss her. Between that and the times she stopped to kiss him, it took nearly twice the time to cover the relatively short distance. Not that she cared. She was riding a wave of euphoria and desire. For the first time in her life, she was free to do whatever she wanted, and tonight, what she wanted most of all was Eric.

She'd never had a lover before. She'd had sex, of course. The hormonal cocktails that drove cyborg aggression also increased their sex drive. During their assessment and basic training period, she'd been with several cyborgs. Later, some of the techs and guards had tried, too, but she'd refused them, even the rare ones that had been kind instead of cruel.

She noted the path they took to his quarters, somehow managing to focus enough to commit the route to memory. It surprised her how close he'd been this whole time, and how much difference a hundred meters made. His quarters were in another section, down a well-lit hall with freshly painted walls. The air had been scrubbed free of the scents that had lingered out in the main concourse, and the silence was almost unnerving after the noise and bustle of the station.

Eric pulled her along with him, both of them laughing as they raced along the corridor, past several doors all marked with names, two of which she recognized – Caldwell and Jessop lived across from each other. "They house all the single officers in the same place?"

"Yeah. I think it's so they can keep us away from the family areas. Less likely we'll corrupt the next generation." Eric grinned. "But since I babysit for Dante and Tyra sometimes, I'm pretty sure I've got that covered."

"I doubt it. I hate to break it to you, but you're not nearly as wicked as you think you are. In fact, you're one of the kindest men I've ever met."

He stopped outside a door, pulling her in for a hard kiss as he slapped his hand down on the scanner to open it. They almost tumbled inside and he spun them around, pressing her up against the wall, his hands on her breasts and the hard ridge of his cock pressed into her stomach. "You think so? Starshine, I'm about to prove you wrong, because I plan on doing terribly wicked things to you tonight."

She shivered, anticipation making her clit throb and her pussy slick with need. "*Veth,* I hope so."

Eric leaned in, stopping just before his lips touched hers. "Tell me you want this."

"I thought I already did." She moved to kiss him, but he shook his head and pulled away a little.

"I want to hear you say the words."

Confusion cooled some of her fire. "Why?"

His lips turned up in a slow, sexy smile that turned her blood to rocket fuel and set it ablaze again. "Let me demonstrate."

He moved closer, his lips tracing a path of delicate kisses from the corner of her mouth, across her cheek, to her ear. "I want you," he whispered. "I want to feel your hands on me as I kiss you. I want you to wrap your legs around my waist as I fuck you. I want to hear my name on your lips when you come."

"Oh," she breathed softly. "Yes, I see."

She turned her head and nuzzled his ear. "I want you, Eric. I want to run my hands over your naked body. I want to hear your sexy whispers in my ear as you fuck me."

He shuddered, a groan tearing loose from his chest as he moved. His lips found hers for a hard, bruising kiss that sent her senses spinning.

"Dress. Off. Now," his words were clipped and bordering on a command. One she was happy to obey.

She placed a hand on his chest, pushing lightly until he stepped back and gave her a little room. In doing so, he finally let her see some of his quarters. They were larger than hers, with a kitchenette as well as one of the standard food dispensers. The color scheme was entirely neutral, soft creams and beiges just like the hall outside. There were a few pieces of furniture, all of them practical, small, and utilitarian. There was a small table with two chairs by the kitchenette, a couch, several large wall monitors all showing starlit skies, and a desk strew with gadgets, tools, two data tablets and a holographic projector that looked like a miniature version of the one she'd seen on the *Malora*.

Before she could see more, Eric moved closer again. Without a word, his hands found her hips, gliding down to her thighs to gather the dress in his hands. He lifted it, and all she had to do was raise her arms as he drew it over her head.

"Holy, hell. Tell me Tyra bought you these or I'm going to need to kill someone."

"The dress?"

"No." Eric's voice was barely more than a low rumble as he gestured at her. "Those."

She glanced down and barely bit back a laugh. Tyra had been right. The tiny scraps of blue lace she'd worn beneath her dress really were designed to make a man lose his mind.

"Of course it was Tyra. Who else could have done it?"

"Don't know. Not feeling very logical right now." He ran a hand through his hair and she took advantage of the moment to step in and untuck his shirt from his pants.

"Clothes off. Now." She did her best to mimic his words and tone.

He chuckled, and in seconds his shirt lay on the floor next to her dress. Then he hauled her back into his arms for another kiss. They continued that way, stripping away their clothes between kisses, fumbling with fasteners and kicking off their shoes without ever losing contact with each other. She touched him everywhere she could, learning his shape, his strength, and tracing the scars that marked his neck and arm. He did the same with her, every caress an exploration, his touch as hungry as it was gentle.

It was his gentleness that broke her, shattering the control she'd held over herself for so long. She'd forgotten what it was like to let go and *feel*.

She let him take the lead, laughing when he lifted her into his arms and carried her to the nearest piece of furniture, his desk. He set her down on one end, then reached past her to sweep the surface clean. There was a clatter as a variety of items fell to the floor but he ignored it, his gaze locked on her face as he parted her legs with his hands and stepped into the space between her thighs.

Without a word he bent to kiss her, his tongue sweeping into her mouth. She started to wrap her legs around his waist but he stopped her with a touch of his hand.

"Not yet," he whispered against her lips as the kiss ended. "We have all night."

"We do." All night. Those words resonated deep inside her. He wanted her to stay with him. Temptations that had nothing to do with her physical need suddenly made themselves known. Companionship. Trust. Security. Love... *No.* She pushed those thoughts away. Ideas like that were foolish and dangerous. She could have this night. Explore her feelings, and create memories that were her own, but that was all she could have.

Eric kissed his way lower, his mouth moving over her skin, whispering compliments and promises of pleasure as he went. This was all that mattered, Their need, their desires. She stroked her fingers threw his dark hair, drawing his head down to her breasts. He caught one tight nipple between his lips and sucked on it while he captured the other peak between his thumb and forefinger, rolling and sucking on them until every other thought fled.

She arched her back and let her head fall back with a soft cry when his teeth found her nipple and closed around it with the lightest of pressure, adding new levels to her pleasure. Her clit pulsed and ached and she reached between them to touch herself, but his hand closed around her wrist.

He placed her hand back on his shoulder before lifting his head. "Your body is mine tonight, Nyx. If you need anything, all you have to do is ask. Tell me what you crave, and I'll give it to you." He tweaked the nipple he still held. "Do you like it when I do that?"

Her breath escaped into a hiss. "Yes."

"But not as much as when I do this." He bowed his head and drew the same nipple into his mouth, biting it gently while flicking the taut nub with the tip of his tongue.

She moaned this time, the sound accompanied by an increased slickness in her pussy.

He lifted his head again. "What else would you like me to do? Maybe put my hand between your legs and play with your clit?" he reached down, sliding a long finger between her folds and moving it in a slow circle around her clitoris.

She shivered and nodded, but he didn't move except to smile wickedly. "Say it, starshine. I want to hear the words."

"I want you to play with my clit. Please. I ache so bad. I need you."

His cock twitched at her words, and she reached for him, wrapping her fingers around his thick length. "You said I couldn't touch myself. But what if I want to touch you?"

He rocked his hips against her hand. "Touch me as much as you like."

She fisted him more firmly and his thighs tensed, the muscles going rigid and his next breath came out in a ragged hiss. He moved, finally, pressing another finger into her pussy to stroke and tease the swollen bundle of nerves buried deep in her folds. She matched his pace and soon they were both panting and wild, riding each other's fingers until she teetered on the edge of orgasm.

When he pulled away, she moaned in protest at the loss of contact, then stilled as he lifted his fingers to his mouth and sucked them clean. "Delicious. I'm going to need more."

Then he was on his knees, his hands on her thighs and his mouth on her pussy. His tongue dove into her folds and he groaned, the vibrations adding new layers of sensation as he found her clit again and sucked it into his mouth.

This time he moved without mercy, his mouth and tongue working together in an oral assault as his fingers slipped into her channel, fucking her with steady strokes that brought her to the brink and sent her hurtling over it into an orgasm that left her gasping for breath like she'd just run the length of the station.

Eric got to his feet and kissed her again, one hand cupping the back of her head, the other low on her back. She could taste herself in that kiss, blended with the warm, spicy notes that were part of Eric.

"Want you too much. Can't wait anymore. Now's the moment you get to wrap those sexy legs around my waist and hold on."

She followed his instructions, arms and legs encircling him, the thick shaft of his cock pressed tantalizingly close to her entrance. She squirmed, inching closer to the edge of the desk and him, then remembered what he'd told her and spoke up. "Need you inside me. Fuck me, Eric. Now."

His dark eyes glittered with pleasure and approval. "I really do love a woman who knows what she wants."

With that, he positioned his cock and pressed into her slowly, her body giving way to his with a delicious sense of fullness that had her flexing her inner walls around him before he was even halfway inside.

When he was finally buried to the hilt inside her, he kissed her again with searing intensity and a single-minded need. He eased her backward until she was lying on the desk, the surface smooth and cool beneath her back. She unwound her arms

She pressed her heels into the top of his glutes as she dropped her hands to the edges of the desk, bracing herself as he began to fuck her with a slow, easy pace she knew was so that she had time to adjust. She didn't need time. She needed *him*.

"Harder. Faster." She lifted her head to smile up at him, "Fuck me, Eric. The way I know you want to."

His fingers sank into her hips, and he uttered a low growl of raw need as he started to move faster, powering into her with thrusts that would have pushed her along the desktop if she hadn't been holding on.

A primal look burned in his gaze as he took her with long, hard strokes that made her body sing and sent sparks sizzling across every nerve. She arched herself off the desktop to meet his thrusts, dizzy with desire and her ragged breathing punctuated with cries of pleasure. They created a music all their own, wild and passionate, the beat set by the slap of flesh meeting flesh and the pounding of her heart.

A new noise started, a harsh scraping sound as the desk began to move across the floor with each of Eric's thrusts. She laughed and held tighter, her fingers sinking into the edges of the desk as her world exploded into silvery shards of pure pleasure.

His name rose from her throat in a wild cry as she came. Her pussy clamped down around him, milking his cock as he continued to move, chasing his own release.

He growled her name on the last thrust, burying himself deep inside her. His cock pulsed and thickened, and he came on a yell that almost drowned out the distinctive sound of something breaking.

The desk canted to one side. She tightened her grip, trying to stop her fall, but the edge snapped off in her hand and she slid toward the floor with her legs still tangled around Eric's waist. They tumbled to the floor in what felt like slow motion. Her landing was cushioned by a floor rug, though they hadn't fallen hard enough to hurt her. Eric was still caught in the thrall of his orgasm, his cock still pulsing inside her as he uttered a strangled laugh.

"That's going to be hard to explain to the quartermaster." His voice was muffled against the crook of her neck.

"Cheap construction," She declared, looking at the desk, which leaned at a drunken angle, two of its legs on the floor a few feet away.

"Clearly." He raised his head to give her a dazed but concerned look. "You okay?"

"Fine. Actually, better than fine. Cyborgs are tough, remember?" She raised a hand to make a languid gesture toward the desk. "Tougher than the furniture, as it turns out." She felt amazing despite the fact they were currently sprawled naked on the floor. She was happy, relaxed, and...content. *So, this is what it feels like. If things were different, I could get used to this.*

"Next time, we'll break the bed. More padding."

"Good plan." She wiggled suggestively beneath him. "Or we could stay here. Can't break the floor."

As TEMPTED as he was to go with her suggestion, Eric opted to untangle himself from Nyx and get to his feet. She took his hand and rose easily, banishing the last of his concerns that she'd been hurt in the fall. They both looked at the remains of his workstation, and Nyx burst into a fit of adorable giggles she kept trying to muffle behind her hand.

He loved seeing her this way, Relaxed, laughing, and gloriously naked. "You're really not hurt? You sure? I could check for bruises and kiss them better if you like."

"I'm pretty sure, but maybe you should check, anyway." She turned her back to him, then glanced back over her shoulder. "Just to be sure."

His mother might not have raised him to be law-abiding, but she'd hadn't raised a fool, either. He had his hands on her shoulders in a heartbeat, pressing a kiss to the back of her head and working his way down from there.

"No bumps on the back of your head," he reported as he moved to her neck, kissing his way across her shoulders and down the graceful lines of her back.

"I thought you were only going to kiss my bruises better."

"I decided to be thorough. After all, I'm not a doctor, and I've only got the one light on. I might miss something."

"Very sensible."

He paused to place a lingering kiss on one perfectly rounded ass cheek. "All good so far, but I think I should keep going."

"Mmhmm," She confirmed with a contented hum that had his cock stirring again as his head filled with images of her making that same sultry sound with her lips wrapped around his dick.

It took a few more minutes to examine the rest of her, all the way down to her ankles, and as he stood again she surprised him by turning and kissing him hard.

He kissed her back, and somehow she was back in his arms again, legs wrapped around his waist as he carried her the short distance to his bedroom.

It was more than an hour later that they finally stopped to rest, limbs tangled, both of them panting, flushed, and sated – at least for the moment.

Nyx trailed her fingers over the raised burn scars

that surrounded the data port on his arm. "How did you get these?"

"Remember when I asked you about V.I.D.A?"

"And you started to mention Absalom, then Dax stopped you and said I hadn't been cleared for that information?"

He cleared his throat. "Yeah. I can't tell you much, but I can tell you a little." He was dancing on the razor's edge of the rules, but she'd been honest with him about her connection to her clone and he wanted to return the favor.

"So, who is she?"

"Not a she, exactly. She's technically an it."

Nyx raised her head from his chest. "She's an it? Explain, please."

"V.I.D.A.," he spelled out the letters this time. "Is short for Virtual Intelligent Digital Assistant. It's an AI program Absalom designed. It was… uh… running a sort of station that the team got sent to for an investigation. V.I.D.A turned out to be the one we were investigating. I was tasked with shutting her down, and she fought back. She attacked me with a power surge that fried some of my implants and came disturbingly close to killing me."

"An AI tried to *kill* you?"

"In her defense, I was trying to do the same to her."

"But, how? I thought there were fail-safes to prevent that from ever happening."

"V.I.D.A was a sentient program, created after

Absalom got special permission to disregard the Pinocchio Protocol."

"*Re'veth*." Her gray eyes widened. "And this AI is still out there?"

Again, he flirted on the edge of what he could say. "No. I managed to destroy her before I blacked out."

"Then why ask me about..." She trailed off. "Ah. You can't say, but I can guess. Absalom was obsessive about backing up all his data. He must have made a copy."

"You have no idea how sexy it is that you're so smart."

She smiled. "You like smart?"

"More than I like chocolate. And that's saying something." A sharp pang of frustration skewered through his good mood. "I wish I could tell you more about what's going on. I think if we could work together, we'd figure out where that asshole is hiding in no time."

"Trust is in short supply these days."

He didn't like the note of unhappiness in her voice, and he gathered her close and rolled over so that she was lying atop him, skin to skin and eye to eye. "I trust you, Nyx. That's not the problem."

"Shh, I know. The problem is the same as it always seems to be. Those who have the power to make decisions covet control, and they don't give it up lightly."

"They really don't. But I'm not letting them control everything."

"No?"

"No. Only two people get to decide if we spend time together. You and me." He had to submit to the rules of the IAF in every part of his life since joining up, but when it came to his personal life, he was drawing a line. Nyx was his choice, and so was whatever they got up to when he was out of uniform.

CHAPTER TEN

"Son of a starbeast. I'm an idiot. Why didn't I think of that before?" Eric exclaimed from the other room, his voice carrying over the sound of the shower she was indulging in. After years of short, tepid showers, the luxury of standing beneath a cascade of hot water had eclipsed almost all other benefits to freedom. Except for the food. The food was incredible.

Over the last few days, Nyx discovered that Eric kept strange hours, waking up in the middle of the night-cycle or early morning to spend time on one of his projects. Sometimes she'd join him, reading or watching vids as he worked. If it was one of his personal projects, she'd ask questions, learning more about robotics and mechanical repairs as he enthusiastically spoke about his various tasks. If he was working on IAF projects, she stayed in bed, giving him privacy so that no one could claim he was breaking security protocols.

This time he was working on IAF matters, so she

had kept her distance, but his exclamation made her curious. She threw on one of Eric's shirts, and went down to the end of the hall, still toweling her hair dry, to see what he was talking about. "What didn't you think of?"

"V.I.D.A." he answered without looking away from the holo-display above his desk.

She checked the time and walked to the food dispenser, her bare feet making no noise as she moved. She'd also learned that when he was distracted, it could take him a few minutes to finish a thought. "I'll make coffee. You're due back on duty in an hour."

"Huh? Oh. Right. Damn. I meant to come back to bed before now." He turned to wink at her. "I really have to get my priorities straight. Beautiful woman in my bed and I'm in another room, chasing data."

"I don't mind. It's nice to have company that sleeps almost as little as I do. So, what did you think of?"

"When I was jacked into the research station where I found you, something about the place felt familiar. Like walking into a room you knew, but hadn't been in for a long time." He gestured to the display. "It was there all along."

"Remember that my expertise is in a very different field than yours, and explain what I'm looking at." She gathered up their mugs and brought them over, setting one down on the desk. He hadn't gotten it replaced, yet. It was propped up with an assortment of spare parts he had on hand, and it looked as if it might fall over at any moment.

"All programs have a distinct fingerprint of a kind. The way their code looks, the way data flows—it all comes together to create a pattern." He pointed to a three-dimensional shape at the center of the display. "Like that."

"Is that a fractal?" she asked.

He nodded. "Cyberspace isn't like the real world. Data has a shape there. Lots of them, actually. It's beautiful. Many of those shapes are fractals, which are really just repeating patterns."

"So, this is what cyberspace looks like?"

"A simplified version. Yeah. That image is what V.I.D.A's pattern looks like."

He reached into the display and pulled out another image. It was incomplete and far simpler than the first one, but she saw the similarities.

"And that?" She took a sip of her drink.

"Is a reconstruction of what I saw inside the research lab's datasphere. Do you see what I see?"

"They could be the same."

"Exactly!" He slapped a hand down on the desk, and it started to tip. "Shit!" He managed to right the desk, and she retrieved his coffee before it fell.

"So, the same program was in both places."

"Yes. You might not have heard anyone mention her, but she was there. That sneaky psychotic bundle of bytes must have vacated the system when the evac was ordered."

"It makes sense. I didn't have much interaction with anyone but my guards and the techs, and we've already conjectured that the guards were likely clones."

"Yeah. You said you didn't see many new faces over the years. It makes sense to clone the low-level staff instead of exposing their operation by hiring outsiders. It's only a theory, though. We won't know for sure until we find them again." He glanced over at her. "Still nothing from your clone?"

She'd sensed…something a few hours ago, a brief whisper that might have been a tentative connection, but it also could have been her imagination. Until she was sure, she didn't see a reason to mention it. "Nothing yet."

"Damn." He leaned back in his chair, rolling his shoulders. "If you sense anything, I think we should tell the team about her."

Over the past few days, she'd learned a lot about Eric, and he knew her better than anyone else in the galaxy. They'd spent almost all their free time together, and while she technically still resided in her own quarters, she spent her nights and evenings at his place. His team seemed fine with it, but there'd been warning rumbles from his superiors about the level of contact. For now, they hadn't interfered, but Nyx knew they would as soon as they had an excuse. Telling them she could sense her clone would give them the reason they needed to separate the two of them, and she wasn't ready to give up Eric. Not yet. "No."

"Why not? It would go a long way toward proving you're on our team. Sharing intel, helping track down these assholes. You want to be part of the team that goes after Absalom, right? This could be how you make that happen."

"Or, it could be the perfect excuse to lock me up and start treating me like a lab experiment. If they think there's a way to track him down, they'll take it, even if it means using me as a tool instead of a human being."

He spun in his chair to face her. "They wouldn't do that. I won't let them."

"Do you really think you could stop them?" She set her mug down on the desktop and folded her arms across her chest. "How?"

"Nova Force isn't like Absalom. They don't treat people that way."

She arched a pale brow. "Says the man who was coerced into joining up to protect his father from prison."

"That's not the same thing. We broke the law."

"And now they limit your access to cyberspace, dictate what projects are acceptable for you to work on. You've kept that device you use to speak to me on my internal channel a secret from them. From everyone. Because you're worried they won't approve. They're not as bad as Absalom and the Gray Men, but they're far from perfect."

"They're the reason you're free right now." His voice came out sharper than she'd heard from him before, and she took a step back.

"Free?" She threw out her arms in frustration to gesture around her. "This is not freedom, Eric. I'm not allowed to leave this area without an escort. My location is constantly monitored, and I spend hours every day answering questions I've already answered hundreds of times. Yesterday I had to undergo another series of scans. As if the dozen or so previous examinations might have missed something, or I could spontaneously grow new implants. Even the med-techs were unhappy that they had to do it again, and they were very kind and apologetic, but it still happened."

"I know. And I'm sorry." He stood up and the air around him crackled with sudden tension. "I don't like it, either. But if you could just give them something that proves your loyalty, then maybe—"

She cut him off with an angry snarl. "My loyalty? I'm not loyal to anyone but myself. I can't be."

"Not even me?"

She was too angry to throttle back on her next words before they were out of her mouth. "Why would I be? Because you rescued me? Because you're kind to me? I'm grateful, but that doesn't mean I'm beholden to you for the rest of my life."

"But we're together!"

"We're sleeping together, yes. At least, we do sometimes, when you're there instead of out here, working one of your projects."

He growled in frustration, one hand running through his hair. "Dammit, Echo, I'm not..." He stopped talking and his mouth fell open for a moment.

"What did you call me?"

"Nyx. Holy *fraxx*, I'm sorry. It's just ... we... I mean

148

she and I had this conversation once, about my leaving the bed in the middle of the night, and I... Dammit, I'm sorry. I know you're not her."

"Stop talking. Just. Stop." She'd known so many kinds of pain in her life, but nothing like this. Her heart had been shredded by his words, leaving her hollow and hurting. She'd let this go on too long, let him get too close. Emotionally compromised. That's what they worried had happened to Eric. *Jokes on them. I'm the one that's compromised. I can't even tell what's real anymore. I let myself take over a dead woman's life.*

"Nyx. I'm sorry."

"So am I." She wanted to say so much more. To berate him. Hurt him. But that wouldn't be fair. He'd never promised her anything. She had the face and form of a woman who had meant something to him, once. He'd told her they weren't the same, but they were clones. Identical. Interchangeable. She'd been living someone else's life, and it was time to end the charade.

"Nyx."

"I need to get dressed."

He moved so he was standing between her and his bedroom. "You need to stay and talk to me. Please." So much emotion packed into a single word. *Please*. Part of her wanted to latch onto the regret in his voice. To forgive. To push it aside so she could pretend a little while longer. That part of her needed to shut up and move on.

"If I'm really free, then only one person gets to

decide what I need to do, and that's me. You don't get a say, Eric."

His next words made it even harder to ignore the part of her that wanted to stay. "You're right. All I can do is ask. The choice is yours." He stepped aside. "So, I'm asking you to stay."

His comms chirped in an undeniably urgent pattern. He cursed. "*Fraxx*. That's Rossi. I have to answer it."

"And I have to get dressed." She walked past him without looking.

She listened in to his conversation while she changed. Her hearing was too good not to hear everything that was said even if she'd closed the door, so she didn't bother with the pretense. Things started out fine, but it only took a few seconds for her to know something was wrong.

"Yes, sir. I'll report to you as soon as—sir? I'm not even dressed—"

Rossi barked something from his side.

"Yessir. I'm on my way."

She'd never heard Eric use so many 'sirs' the entire time she'd known him. Something was happening. Something serious.

He flew into the room seconds later, grabbing a fresh uniform out of the closet with one hand as he tore his t-shirt off with the other. Any other day, she'd have enjoyed the view, But no. She wasn't going to ogle him. That was over, too.

"Trouble?" She asked as she tugged on her shoes. She hadn't planned on saying anything, but the words came out anyway. Probably a short circuit caused by all that sculpted muscle on display.

He gave her a strained look. "I can't say anything. Orders."

Her anger came back, stronger than ever. "He ordered you not to talk to me. These are the people you think I should trust?"

"Nyx, wait. I have to go, but we still need to talk. Later?"

She brushed past him without looking his way or saying anything. There was nothing left to say.

"Nyx!"

"Report to your commander, Ensign. He didn't sound like a man that should be kept waiting." She managed to keep her tone cool and level, and if there were hot tears on her cheeks as she walked out the door, there was no one around to see. She was alone, which was how it had to be.

CHAPTER ELEVEN

FRAXX. Fraxx. Fraxx!

He'd screwed up with Nyx on a galactic scale. Worse than that, he'd hurt her. He'd seen that in her eyes before she'd retreated behind her emotional walls. How could he have been that stupid?

He scrubbed a hand over his face. He was tired, true. And he'd been too focused on the mission to pay proper attention to her, or to what he was saying. Worse, he couldn't fix it, yet, because he was being ordered to report to HQ on the double. In fact, Dax had implied that if he wasn't there fast enough, someone would come looking for him. What the hell was going on? And why now? *"Fraxx!"*

He shut down his system and secured all his files before leaving, then jogged the entire way to Dax's office. An office he'd only been to once since they'd moved. Dax preferred to run most of the day to day business from the briefing rooms.

He made it in good time, his thoughts racing faster than his feet as he tried to figure out what the hell he was going to do to fix things with Nyx, along with working out why Dax wanted to see him so early in the morning. He didn't have answers to either question by the time he arrived, which meant he'd be walking into Dax's office blind. Not his preferred scenario.

He took a second to tug his uniform into place, and activated the door chime to announce his presence. Dax wasn't much for protocol, and on any other day he'd have walked right in, but something told him today wasn't the day to do anything casually.

"Ensign Erben reporting as ordered, sir."

"Enter."

Not good. No words of welcome. Dax hadn't even used his name. He squared his shoulders, lifted his head, and opened the door to face whatever new hell the universe had decided to send his way.

Dax's office was relatively spacious by station standards, but today it was packed.

Dax was at his desk. Standing beside him, his arms folded across his puffed-out chest in what was clearly supposed to be a power pose, was a man Eric hadn't seen before. He was lean, with a hawk-like profile, close-cropped brown hair that showed gray at the temples, and a thin-lipped mouth that was currently set in an unpleasant little sneer.

"Good of you to finally join us, Ensign."

Eric came to attention and snapped off a textbook

perfect salute. "Sir. I came as soon as I received the summons, sir."

Dax kept his features neutral, but Eric could tell his commander was not pleased with the way this meeting had started. The – he checked the man's insignia and cursed inwardly – the new arrival was a Brigadier General, and he was clearly not in a mood to follow polite protocol like introductions.

His commander got to his feet. "Ensign Erben, this is Brigadier General Halverson and his aide de camp, Lieutenant Clooney. They're here to review and to address some concerns raised regarding the operations of the Nova Force teams in this sector."

He waded through Dax's formal phrasing and came to an unpleasant conclusion. There was only one team assigned to this sector - theirs. Which meant Halverson and his lackey were here to poke their noses into team three's business. Could this day get any worse?

Dax went on to identify the others in the room. Colonel Scott Archer, the ranking IAF officer for the station, and his aide, a demure young woman in a dark suit instead of an IAF uniform that Dax introduced only as Penny. "And you know Colonel Bahl, head of Nova Force. She is attending via hologram."

He nodded to each person as they were introduced but stayed quiet. Once that courtesy had been seen to, Dax pushed his chair aside and remained standing. That was when Eric noticed that his commander was at least four inches taller than Halverson.

"At ease, Ensign," Dax said a moment later.

"For now," Halverson added.

Dax frowned. It was a minute expression, but Eric caught it. His commander was losing patience with Halverson, but given his rank, there wasn't a damned thing anyone could do about it. Rank really did have its privileges.

His commander cleared his throat, then spoke. "You've been called to this meeting because there are allegations being made against you, Ensign Erben, regarding your recent conduct."

"Sir? I'm not sure what conduct you could be referring to." This couldn't be about Nyx, could it? Had she been right all along? The list of things he needed to apologize for was getting longer by the minute.

"Let me refresh your memory, Ensign." Halverson nodded to his aide, who tapped the data tablet in his hand. A second later a hologram shimmered into existence in the air over Dax's desk.

Eric's stomach twisted as he saw what was being displayed. There was a vid-capture of him jacked into the data node he'd used the day he'd sent his sprites – his very illegal sprites – out into cyberspace to look for Nyx. There was more, too, but the more he read, the more confused he got. It showed that someone using his codes had attempted to hack into the IAF system more than once over the last week, but the techniques they used were messy, outdated, and doomed to fail. There were black market inquiries about new identities and several offers to sell IAF data to a winning bidder, but again it was all crudely done, worded in such a way that even the most basic review would flag the communique with every law enforcement group in the galaxy.

"Look familiar?" the general drawled, looking smug.

"No, sir."

"What?" Halverson barked.

"I recognize one thing in that collection, sir." He pointed to the vid-capture of him. "That did happen, sir. But it occurred more than a month ago."

"Not according to the date stamp." Halverson pointed. "Right there. And I had it verified. This shows you were committing a breach of this station's systems two days ago, which matches the dates on some of the other evidence, and it's all been verified, too."

He fought to stay in control of his mouth, and his temper, but some of his anger at being accused of betraying Nova Force and his oath of service bled into his next words. "Respectfully, sir. Whoever verified that data is an idiot. I am a loyal officer of the IAF and a proud member of Nova Force. I would not, under any circumstances, betray my oath or my teammates by selling IAF secrets."

The aide pressed his mouth into a disapproving line so tight his lips almost disappeared. *And now I know which idiot verified the images.*

"But you *do* admit to breaking your agreement with the IAF and going into cyberspace without oversight or orders," Halverson pressed on.

"Yes, sir." There was no point in denying it. All he

could do was make sure that no one ever learned that Kurt had known and didn't report it.

"And there we have it. Commander Rossi, have this man arrested. I'll see to the paperwork discharging him from service, and he can join his father on Tantalus Four. Maybe we can find them adjoining cells." Halverson glanced over at his aide. "I assume his accomplice is already in custody?"

"No, sir. She is not. I have no record of the cyborg female being held in custody anywhere in the complex."

They thought *Nyx* was involved in this mess? He was on the verge of defending Nyx when Colonel Bahl spoke up. "The ensign's father has served his time and is now a free citizen of the galaxy. Whatever happens, his situation will not be affected by Ensign Erben's fate."

Halverson huffed. "Fine. The father was a minor concern, anyway. We have our main suspect right here."

"And while the ensign has admitted to breaking the agreement, I must respectfully point out that his probation period has long since ended," Dax spoke up next, his voice carefully neutral. "And while the other accusations against him are serious, that is all they are right now, accusations. Ensign Erben is entitled to a fair hearing, legal representation, and a chance to defend himself against these allegations. Furthermore, Nyx has been granted all the rights and privileges of a guest."

"On whose authority?" the general demanded.

"She's a hostile asset at best, and potentially an enemy agent sent here to spy on us."

"My authority, sir," Dax declared.

"With my approval," Bahl added.

A fierce sense of gratitude filled him at his commander's words. Dax wasn't going to let this arrogant ass railroad him or Nyx. He was still in a freighter full of trouble, but none of the more serious charges would stick once they'd been reviewed by an expert. Anyone with more than a cursory understanding of cybercrimes and data manipulation would recognize that Halverson's so-called evidence had been faked.

Someone was trying to sideline him, and they were using the Brigadier General to do it. Worse, someone was trying to set up Nyx.

"I want her contained. Now," Halverson stated.

"She is contained, sir. She volunteered to wear a tracking device. We know where she is at all times," Dax pointed out.

"She's a high-level security risk with known links to our enemy, and you're letting her wander around like a *fraxxing* pet?"

"She's not a—"

Archer drowned him out, the colonel's voice carrying far more command than Halverson had managed. "Sir. I respectfully remind you that the cyborg known as Nyx is a free citizen of the galaxy under the Unified Galactic Agreement, and as such is entitled to—"

"She's an assassin and an agent of the enemy. No wonder I was sent out here—three ranking officers and you're all acting as if that abom— that female - is just another citizen to be protected."

Eric was certain the general was about to refer to Nyx as an abomination, which explained a great deal about the man's behavior. It was common knowledge that not everyone was open to the idea that the cyborgs, beings who had been created by the corporations to fight in their 'bloodless' war, should have ever been granted citizenship. There were those who saw them as chattel, objects that could be used and discarded. Disposable soldiers. If the general held those kinds of opinions, then he'd see Nyx as… damn it. He'd see Nyx as a tool to be used any way he deemed necessary. If he got his hands on her, she'd have all the proof she needed that she was right, and she'd never trust them again. He'd lose her. If he hadn't already.

Colonel Bahl spoke, her voice far quieter than Archer's, but it carried the same weight of command. "General Halverson. You are outside my chain of command, and therefore outside the command structure of Nova Force. As such, I feel I must remind you, respectfully, that your authority is limited to investigation and review. No action can be taken until you submit your final report to those who sent you here."

No one spoke for a long moment. Bahl had come so close to crossing the line you could measure the room she had left in nanometres.

"Then I will proceed with my investigation." The general pointed to Eric. "I want his quarters searched. Commander Rossi, you will see to it that every piece of tech the ensign owns, has access to, or so much as looks at is seized and inspected for any evidence of wrongdoing. My aide will hand over copies of all the evidence we already have to be re-verified, and I want Ensign Erben escorted to an interrogation room immediately. Oh, and find the cyborg and have her brought in for questioning, too."

Dax turned to acknowledge the general's order with a salute that was a half-second too slow to be perfect. "Yes, sir. The ensign will be delivered to interrogation for questioning as soon as a JAG officer is made available to represent him."

"I'll see to it," Archer said.

"Thank you, Colonel." Divya nodded to Archer, then turned her holographic form to address the general. "I will arrange for all of your evidence to be reviewed at Nova Force Headquarters. That should address any concerns you might have as to bias, General Halverson. Will that be all?"

He waved a hand. "Yes. Fine. My aide will send you the pertinent files shortly."

It was painfully obvious to everyone in the room that Halverson was livid, but there was nothing he could do about it. Protocol was paramount, and while his rank allowed him a great deal of latitude, he couldn't blatantly ignore it without destroying the credibility of the investigation. He had to play by the rules.

"Thank you, sir. I'll await the files." Bahl nodded to Rossi, then gave Eric a smaller nod before her hologram disappeared.

Archer departed next, edging out of the crowded room with his aide a few steps behind him.

"One more thing," Halverson said once the others were gone.

"Yes, sir?" Dax asked.

"See to it that there is no contact between the cyborg and the ensign. I don't want them to have time to coordinate their stories."

Eric managed to hold his temper until the door closed.

"*Fraxx*!" he growled, still careful to keep his voice low in case Halverson was lingering outside.

"I'll need your communicator, Ensign." Dax ordered, but he softened the tone with a slight smile and raised a finger to his lips.

"Yes, sir." Eric walked over and placed his comms on the desk with enough noise to be sure it carried to anyone who might be listening in. As he did it, Dax placed a portable privacy-field generator on the table and flicked it on with a swipe of a finger. The air around them shimmered, visible proof they could now talk without being overheard.

"*Fraxxing* hell, Magi. I know our unofficial motto is no feather left unruffled, but that's supposed to apply to the bad guys, not the brass! Care to tell me what you were doing sneaking around hacking into unused data nodes?"

"I was looking for Nyx."

Dax sighed. "So, that's how you managed to track down the research lab. You went to the dark side."

"I *visited* the dark side. Briefly. Haven't you heard? They have the best cookies."

Dax shot him a look that was two parts annoyance and one part amusement. "Still with the jokes. You are up to your elbows in trouble, and still, jokes."

"It's my default setting."

"Well, stow it. You start mouthing off to Halverson and he'll find a way to make something stick."

"I know. It's just... this has been an exceptionally shit day and it's barely started. I need to get my head straight."

"And fast. I don't know who pointed the general our way, but there's more going on here then we can see."

"Yeah. I think, maybe, V.I.D.A is involved somehow. This feels like her kind of play, leaking information, setting up discord. We've seen her do it before."

"V.I.D.A was terminated, and will you stop calling that bundle of code a she? You're in enough trouble without making people question your sanity, too."

"I found something today that proves V.I.D.A's software was present on the research station. Problem is, that proof is on the computer that's probably being seized in the next few minutes."

Dax swore. "You think Halverson is involved?"

"No idea. But him arriving now, right as I'm putting the pieces together? Someone had to have put all this in motion days ago. Which means either it's a massive coincidence…"

"Or someone's playing with us, and they're planning six moves ahead." Dax grunted. "And that *does* sound like V.I.D.A."

"The question is, how the *fraxx* did she—I mean it—know about Nyx?

"The same way they knew we were headed for the station. The Grays have a spy planted somewhere." Dax checked the time. "You don't have long. Anything else I need to know?"

"Yeah. Uh. But it's a personal issue."

"And it's relevant now?"

"It could be."

Dax sighed. "What happened?"

"I fraxxed up with Nyx. Like, supernova levels of kaboom."

What did you do?"

"I called her Echo."

Dax winced. "Ouch."

"We were arguing about Nova Force and who she could trust. She doesn't have faith in anyone but the team, really. I told her she was wrong…" He gestured around them. "But I'm the one who was wrong, and now I can't even warn her. I need you to get a message to her. Tell her what's happened and that you've got her back. Please? Because I'm not going to be able to help her, not for a while, anyway."

"You got it. We'll take care of her. You have my word."

He exhaled and one of the knots in his guts loosened a little. "Thank you. And thank you for doing what you could to derail the general today. If he'd had his way…"

"You'd be in a cell, and Nyx would probably be being prepped for transport off the station. Yeah. I noticed that. Like I said, there's more here then what we can see, and I don't like it. Someone's messing with my team." Dax straightened and laid a hand on his shoulder. "My family."

Eric opened his mouth and Dax cut him off with a slash of his hand. "One daddy joke out of you and I'll hand your ass over to the general myself."

"No daddy jokes. Got it." Eric lightly slapped Dax's hand where it sat on his shoulder. "But thank you."

"But since we're family, and no one can hear us right now, I'm going to give you a little advice."

He shrugged off Dax's hand and stepped away from his friend. "I know what you're going to say. Stay away from Nyx. But I can't do that." The idea of letting go of Nyx made his heart hurt. He didn't want to lose her.

Dax snorted. "Of course you can't. You're falling for her."

Eric spoke before his brain caught up to his mouth. "No. I mean. Maybe. Yes?" *Fraxx.* Was Dax right? He'd been enjoying their time together. She challenged him, made him laugh, and when she smiled at him, the whole universe vanished except for her. He'd *fraxxed* up and called her Echo, but that had been a thoughtless slip of the tongue. She was the original, the source code, and there was no comparing her or mistaking her for anyone else.

"And that word-salad of confusion is all the confirmation I need. So, ready for that advice now?"

"Uh. Yes. Because I have no idea how to fix things with her, and she's going to be even more pissed now because everything she tried to warn me about is happening." He threw up his hands in frustration. "I already apologized. She didn't want to hear it."

Dax sat on the edge of his desk. "Yeah. Apologies are nice, but they're only the first step. You need to tell her."

"I'm not even allowed to talk to her right now. And tell her what? You just said apologizing won't be enough."

"You can't talk to her yet, but we'll get this mess sorted out. Then, you need to tell her how you feel. I didn't do that, and it cost me years with the woman I love. Dante was in denial, too, and he nearly died before he could fix it. So, that's my advice. Tell her."

He could do that. Maybe bring a present. Flowers. Make her dinner. Show her she mattered. Yeah. "Okay."

Dax turned off the privacy field and dropped the device back into his pocket. "Then take a seat and start thinking about what you're going to tell the JAG officer when they get here. While you do that, I'll send Buttercup to track down Nyx. He can explain what's going on while he's bringing her in for questioning. I'm going to assign Blink to monitor her interrogation, and Sabre will sit in on yours."

Which meant Dax wanted both of them to have a friendly face in the room. An ally who could make sure that things stayed above board.

"Thank you, sir."

"Don't thank me. Just show your gratitude by making sure you don't piss off anyone else for a while. Less paperwork for me that way."

"Yes, sir." He already had enough people angry at him, and one of them was a *fraxxing* assassin. His dance card was full and he hadn't had breakfast, yet. It was time to focus on what was important: getting out of here, and talking to Nyx.

CHAPTER TWELVE

IT WAS a short walk from Eric's quarters to hers, but she ran into several IAF personnel along the way. The day cycle was starting, and people were heading to the gym or the common room to grab a meal and some conversation before they went on duty. She didn't recognize anyone, and it struck her that apart from Eric and his team, she had no connections to anyone on the station. She was almost as alone here as when she was a prisoner. In some ways, she was even more so because back then she'd been linked to her clones. Being with Eric had distracted her from the truth of her situation. She was still a prisoner, still isolated and on her own.

Her time with Eric had been an enjoyable escape, but that's all it could be. She needed to finish her mission. Find Absalom, destroy him, and end the Fury Project forever. If he had any more of her clones, she'd free them, but her main goal was to take down the one man who had used her as a test subject for years. He had to pay for what he'd done.

Focus. That's what she'd been missing. She'd lost sight of her goals. She concentrated on her anger, letting it push aside all thoughts of Eric and the hurt he'd caused with his verbal slip. She let herself remember the years of captivity. The petty torments, the tests, the loneliness. She had to make sure Absalom never did this to anyone else. She was the original, the source of all their suffering, and it was up to her to put an end to it, for all of them.

She walked through her door and engaged the locks behind her. She looked around the sparsely furnished room and saw nothing that would work for what she wanted to do, so she turned off her comms, set it aside, sat cross-legged on the floor and closed her eyes. She slowed her breathing, centered her thoughts as best she could, and focused on the one person she still wanted to hear from.

"Where are you? Why haven't I felt your presence?" She'd never attempted to create a connection. She wasn't sure she could do it at all, and she hadn't dared to try before, not when her every move was being monitored by Absalom and his techs.

She tried again, reaching out blindly, pouring all her thoughts and emotions into forming a link, but there was nothing. Again and again she tried, only giving up when her frustration grew so great she couldn't focus anymore.

Feeling more alone than ever, she got to her feet and

stretched. She couldn't stay here. The walls were already closing in on her, the spartan space feeling too much like the cell she'd left behind. She needed to move. To do something... but she couldn't leave the area without an escort, and she didn't want to see any of Eric's friends right now. She might have called Tyra, but she was working at the med-center today, and to reach it she'd need an escort.

"*Fraxx!*" She smacked her hand into the nearest wall without thinking, and the impact left a sizable dent in the reinforced steel. And that gave her an idea. She'd head to the gym and beat up Bessy the spar-bot. She hadn't worked out properly in a few days, and while sex with Eric certainly counted as cardio, today she needed the satisfaction of hitting something.

She changed into one of the few outfits left in her quarters, a simple set of workout gear marked with the Nova Force logo. It was the same one she'd been wearing the first time Trinity had brought her to the gym...and to Eric.

She bent over to tighten her shoes and nearly fell forward as familiar pain flared across her temples. Contact!

"*You are alive!*" the thought streaked through her mind like a comet.

She sent back a confirming thought. She'd learned that emotions were easier to convey than specific words.

The fury responded with an outpouring of thoughts and feelings that was almost impossible to understand.

She gritted her teeth against the pain and pushed a single thought back. *"Calm."*

The torrent became a stream, then a trickle, and finally a pair of simple questions. *"How? Where?"*

"Nova Force. Free."

"Free?" The thought was sent with a surge of joy mixed with a bittersweet sense of longing.

"Absalom?"

"Here with him."

"Where here?" Nyx added layers of urgency to the query, hoping her clone would understand. Keeping a connection open for long was difficult, and neither one of them would be able to maintain it for much longer.

There was no response, but the link between them still held. She knelt on the floor, her head aching, and waited.

"Where?" She asked again.

Instead of emotions or words, her clone answered with an image. *Clever.* Cyborgs could store memories as if they were data. She'd gotten flashes of her clone's lives before, but none of the furies had ever deliberately sent her an image this way. It wasn't much, but at the same time, it was everything. The image showed part of a data screen. Part of it was blocked by the body of a person standing between the clone and the monitor, but there were numbers visible. Coordinates.

Yes! Elation filled her. She had what she needed to put an end to this. No more furies. No more suffering. She could stop Absalom and fulfill her promise to the ones whose lives he'd stolen.

She managed to send a brief sense of gratitude to her clone before the link broke and she was alone inside her head once more. She'd missed that sense of connection, though she didn't miss the pain that came with it. Eric had a theory that her ability to connect to her clones was a kind of limited telepathy, similar to the bond between naturally born twins, only stronger. He'd sent her several articles documenting the phenomenon in other vat-born cybernetic clones, but the information was sparse, mostly anecdotal reports from technicians. If it was deemed minor, the cyborgs were sent off to fight, if there were any concerns, the subjects were flagged as failures and decommissioned.

Nyx fastened her shoes before standing up and taking stock of what little she owned. There wasn't much. A data tablet, communicator, some toiletries, and a handful of clothing.

She grabbed the tablet and entered the coordinates. She needed to know where Absalom was so she could make a plan. Weapons. Supplies. A ship. How long would it take her to reach him?

The answer stunned her, and she had to double-check before she believed it. The arrogant bastard was close. According to her clone, she and Absalom were somewhere in the asteroid field beyond the Drift. He must be laughing, knowing he was less than two days travel from the people hunting him.

"You won't be laughing soon," she vowed.

She packed a small bag with toiletries and the data tablet, then considered her options. She needed more gear. Weapons, if she could find some, and a ship. A voice in the back of her mind whispered that if she told Eric what she'd learned, he'd make sure she had everything she needed. But talking to him meant…well, talking to him.

She scoffed aloud, amused and annoyed with herself. She was starting to see why the corporations had done their best to repress their cyborg soldiers' emotions – it made things messy and illogical, and she didn't have time for either.

Eric's quarters were one of the few places she could go without attracting attention, though, and he had equipment there, including his spare blaster. He should be on duty for hours, which would give her plenty of time.

That plan held until she turned down the hallway to Eric's place and saw an IAF soldier stationed outside his open door. The hall was half-blocked by a stack of computer equipment, all of it Eric's. *Fraxx*.

She ducked back around the corner, cursing softly. A quick check of the area confirmed she was alone in this part of the hallway, so she took a chance and stayed where she was, extending her senses in an attempt to find out what she could.

"You almost done?" A male voice asked.

"Just doing one more pass. This guy has more gizmos and tech in his place than some of the stores on the concourse."

"Yeah. I heard he's some kind of cyber-jockey. Tech is his thing."

There was a snort of laughter from inside. "That would explain his girlfriend. You hear he's dating a cyborg?"

"I heard they're working together. General Halverson wants her for questioning as soon as he's done with the ensign."

"You think he did what they're saying he did?" The one who had been inside must have stepped into the corridor, because his voice was clearer now.

"I doubt it. He's Nova Force for *fraxx* sake."

"So? Everyone's got their price."

"That's not what I meant. Nova Force are experts at finding out what the corporations are doing. Espionage, data theft, that kind of thing. If one of them went rogue, they'd know exactly how to do it to make sure they weren't caught. And Erben is a cyber-jockey. He's literally wired to be good at this kind of shit. So, how'd they catch him so easily? This doesn't feel right, know what I mean?"

She'd heard enough. Nyx turned and went back the way she'd come, her thoughts racing along at light-speed. Eric was in trouble, and they thought she was working with him. She couldn't go to him for help, and she couldn't do anything to get him out of trouble, either. *Dammit.* This was exactly what she'd been trying to warn him about.

She needed a new plan. She already knew the first step. The tracker on her wrist needed to come off, right now. She tried to twist it, but it was snug against her flesh and there wasn't any way for her to get the leverage she needed. A door opened up ahead and she froze, every muscle primed and ready to react if a threat appeared.

A squat maintenance bot trundled out into the hall, polishing the floor. She darted forward, managing to get her foot in the way of the door as it slid closed. It sensed the obstruction and re-opened, giving her just enough time to slip inside the small maintenance room before the door closed behind her.

The only light source was a faint glow from a control panel on one wall, where indicator lights in various colors marked the progress of the fleet of maintenance bots assigned to this area. She shifted her eyes to low-light mode, and was able to see well enough to find what she needed. The bots could multitask, selecting various attachments set near their recharging bays to suit their assigned tasks. She grabbed the first one that looked like it would suit her needs and slipped the metal tab between the tracker and her wrist. It hurt, but physical pain was something she could deal with. She simply deactivated her pain receptors and kept going, trusting in her medi-bots to manage any injuries she inflicted on herself. It took more force than she expected to snap the tracker's band, but it came off eventually, leaving her with a bruised and bloodied wrist.

She wiped away the blood with one of her shirts while she considered where to leave the tracker. A bot whirred to life at her feet, and she grinned. Perfect. She grabbed the bot before it could zip away on its next assignment, holding it off the ground until she found a way to fasten the tracker to it. It chittered in mild alarm at being handled, and by the time she found a niche to wedge the tracker into, the bot was beeping at her in what could only be annoyance. The moment she set it down it stopped complaining, made a series of low, pulsing warbles and zoomed off.

She waited for a ten-count, mentally reviewing what she knew about the layout of the station. She needed a ship, which meant she had to get to either the docking spars or the repair bays. The spars would be full of functioning ships, but they would also be bustling with activity and the ships would all be secured against theft. If she went for a ship under repairs, she'd have a better chance of getting away with stealing transport, albeit one with dubious performance.

Given that she didn't have far to travel, she opted for availability over reliability. Her basic programming had included piloting, basic ship maintenance, and repairs. If she picked the right vessel, she'd reach Absalom. That was her only goal.

She'd have to take the long way, which meant making her way through the maze of maintenance tunnels and shafts that honeycombed the station. She placed her comm unit on one of the re-charging bots, slung her bag over her shoulder, checked to make sure her injured wrist wasn't too noticeable, and slipped back into the corridor. Whatever ship she stole, it better have a working shower. By the time she made it through the tunnels, she was going to need it.

Waiting quietly was not a skill Eric had ever mastered. The interrogation room he was in was empty save for himself, Kurt, a couple of chairs, and a battered steel table that looked like it had been recently liberated from the mess hall.

"Magi, if you don't stop bouncing your foot on the floor, I'm going to do something you won't enjoy and will leave you limping for days. You're innocent, remember? Innocent men are calm, collected, and do not twitch like they mainlined ja'kreesh for breakfast," Kurt reminded him gruffly.

He stilled his mind and his body, leaning back in his chair and unclenching his hands.

Kurt grunted. "Better. You know who JAG is sending over?"

"No. Archer—I mean Colonel Archer only said he'd get someone over here."

Kurt raised a brow at his slip but didn't say anything. He was the lead interrogator for Team Three, and he'd been training Eric in the art for months. Every word and gesture mattered when trying to determine guilt, and Eric had been sloppy. He needed to stop worrying about Nyx and focus on his current problem.

There was a light knock at the door, and it opened a second later to reveal a curvy woman with dark hair and a professional smile standing in the doorway. She was average height, but there was nothing average about the way she walked into the room, confidently assessing everyone in it with a single glance.

Normally, she was exactly the kind of woman he liked. Sure, capable, with just a hint of danger hiding under the surface. And yet, all he felt was relief that Archer had sent someone competent. Kurt's reaction was a lot more interesting. He sucked in a sharp breath, then went still.

"Good day. I'm Lieutenant Commander Castille, Judge Advocate General's Corps. Colonel Archer asked me to represent you today, Ensign Erben. Do you agree to have me present during this questioning period?"

She shot a hard look at Kurt. "You haven't started questioning him already have you?"

"I'm happy to have you here today, Lieutenant Commander, please join us." He nodded to Kurt. "This is Lieutenant Commander Meyer, a teammate from Nova Force. He's here to uh…" He wasn't quite sure how to explain Kurt's role.

Kurt stepped into the conversation. "I'm here to answer any questions General Halverson might have about how our team functions, and how our methods differ from standard IAF protocol on some matters."

"Ah." Castille's smile widened into something warmer for a moment. "Ally in the room?"

Kurt nodded and gave her a ghost of a smile. "Something like that."

The JAG officer barely had time to take a seat and take out a data tablet before the door opened again, this time without any warning. The General barged in, and it was obvious before he'd taken two steps into the room what his tactics would be – bluster and bravado.

"Why isn't this man in restraints?" he demanded. Then he turned his gaze on the two officers flanking Eric. "And who are you people?"

All three of them stood as the General took a seat at the table. He was alone, which meant that his aide was elsewhere. Probably keeping an eye out for Nyx when they brought her in. Had Dante told her what was happening? Did she know what she was walking into?

Kurt and Castille introduced themselves and everyone took their seats again.

Halverson laid into Eric the second his ass touched the chair. "Why'd you do it, Ensign?"

"Sir? I'm not sure what you're referring to."

"You admitted to committing cybercrimes and acting against the IAF. I want to know why."

Castille held up a hand and looked at him. "I see nothing in my notes about that. Did you admit to either of those offenses, Ensign?"

"No, Lieutenant Commander, I did not."

She turned back to the General, her expression calm and cool. "Perhaps if you rephrased your question, General."

Halverson's jaws tightened. "Very well, since the ensign seems to be having difficulty understanding my very simple question, I'll reword it for him. You've already admitted to committing this breach of security. I want to know why, and what information you were after."

Eric picked his words carefully. "During my investigation into the existence of Project Fury, I found myself up against an adversary who excelled at wiping data and deleting any evidentiary trail I tried to follow. This adversary was not bound by the same rules as I was, and as such, was more successful in their efforts. Eventually, I realized that if I was going to beat this being, I'd have to break the rules."

"By attacking the IAF? How did that further your investigation, exactly?"

"I never attacked the IAF, sir. Whatever proof you have that I did, it's been falsified, just like the date stamp on the security footage you have of me."

Halverson's next salvo of stupidity was halted by a brisk knock at the door, one that fell into an unusual pattern. Two knocks, then one, then two more.

"Come in, Lieutenant Clooney," the general called, already turning in his chair.

The lieutenant came in, looking unhappy and agitated. He leaned down to murmur a message to Halverson and handed him something metallic.

The general exploded. "Find her! I don't care if it takes every IAF soldier stationed here and they have to search every level of this starsforsaken station, I want her in custody before lunch."

"Of course, sir. A search is already underway." The aide nodded, turned crisply, and departed without another word. Halverson spun to face Eric again and bellowed, "Where is she?"

"Who, sir?" It had to be Nyx, and he didn't know

whether to be happy or worried that she'd slipped away. Was she alright? Why had she run? And where the hell would she go?

"Don't play coy with me. You know who. Your cyborg accomplice. Where is she?" Halverson slapped his hand down on the table, and when he withdrew it, he left Nyx's tracker lying on the table. It was mangled and broken, and there were traces of blood smeared across its smooth band. She'd gotten it off, but at a cost.

"I have no idea, sir. When I left my quarters to answer Commander Rossi's summons she had already left. I have been here since then, and by your own orders I have had no contact with anyone except the Commander and Lieutenant Commanders Meyer and Castille."

"She's your accomplice! Surely you know where she would go. This was found on a maintenance bot not far from your quarters. She can't have gotten far."

"She's not my accomplice, sir. My only act of disobedience was done in order to locate a hostile entity with links to the Gray Men. Nyx is a victim of that same entity and has done nothing wrong." At least, she hadn't done anything wrong until now. If she'd ditched the tracker, then she knew they were looking for her. She could be anywhere on the station by now, and probably looking to get off Astek as soon as possible.

"It's all very convenient, isn't it, though? You just happen to find information leading to a secret base, but all you manage to bring back is next to useless scraps of data and a cyborg with enemy affiliations. That female was then released and allowed to roam free to gather information and report back to her masters. Either you're part of this conspiracy, or you've been played for a fool. Which is it?"

Eric didn't respond. He saw the trap Halverson had laid for him, and he wasn't stepping into it.

After an uncomfortably long silence, Halverson pushed back his chair. "Are you refusing to answer my questions, now, Ensign?"

"No, sir. I thought your last question was rhetorical, sir."

The general got to his feet. "You and I are not done, Ensign. Not by a long shot. I'm going to find out what's being done to find your partner in crime. Once she's in custody, I'll have more questions for you."

Eric nodded in understanding and the General stalked out a moment later. Once he was gone, all three relaxed a little.

"Do I want to know what all that was really about?" Castille asked.

"No idea. As interrogations go that was… unique," Kurt said.

"Someone wants me sidelined so they can go after Nyx and I think they're using the general to do it."

"Using a general? Isn't that a complicated way to make things happen?" Castille asked.

Kurt grunted. "You must be new here. The Grays love complex plots. Makes it hard to figure out what's really going on, and who is to blame."

"I got here about a month ago. Until today most of

what I've been handling were minor issues, clashes between the regulars and our personnel. I don't know much about these Grays... I'm assuming you mean the Gray Men?"

"Yeah. If you're going to be defending Erben, you're going to need more information. I'll arrange for a briefing to get you up to speed. What's your security clearance?"

Castille smiled. "That's a rather sensitive question, Lieutenant Commander."

"I'd ask you out for a drink first, but we're pressed for time. Maybe later?"

Eric watched the byplay with a mixture of amusement and annoyance. His life was falling apart and Kurt was taking time out to flirt?

Her smile widened. "Later, then. And I'm cleared for Tier Four – Black."

Both men stared. She had a higher clearance than they did. What the hell kind of work was she doing for JAG to need that?

"Well then, a full briefing shouldn't be a problem." Kurt got to his feet, then leaned over to pick up the tracker Halverson had left on the table. "So, Nyx is injured and on the run. Any idea where she might be headed, Magi?"

"She took that off near my place, which means she probably went back there to get her things while I was gone, spotted whoever was sent to seize my equipment, and realized she'd been right all along and I was a bigger idiot than she already thought."

Kurt's brows hit his hairline. "*Fraxxing* hell. What did you do?"

Eric summarized the morning's events as briefly as possible. He didn't enjoy it any more the second time he had to explain it, but it gave him an idea. "I don't know where she is, but I might be able to find out. Am I free to return to my quarters?"

"Your quarters, yes. But I wouldn't advise going much farther than that. Halverson made it clear he wants you close by." Castille stood, placed her data tablet in her bag, and looked at them both. "Be careful what you say and do for the next few days, Ensign, and if you're called in again, I want you to contact me right away."

They exchanged contact information, shook hands, and parted company.

"So, what's in your quarters?"

"Something that's going to get me in more trouble, but if I'm going to find Nyx, I need it. It would probably be best if you weren't with me, though."

Kurt didn't look happy, but he didn't argue. "I hate these games we have to play. Go, do what you need to do, then meet me back here. Rossi's office. We'll come up with a plan."

"I'll be back as soon as I can." He clapped Kurt on the shoulder. "And thanks for having my back today."

"Thanks for having mine." Eric could have saved himself at least some trouble if he'd revealed that Kurt knew what he'd done to find Nyx. He'd never do that, though.

"Any time."

Kurt nodded. "See you in a few."

It wouldn't take long to get back to his quarters. If he was lucky, then the device he'd built would still be safe in it's hiding spot and he'd be able to contact Nyx. The way his day had gone so far, he was due for a change in fortune...wasn't he?

CHAPTER THIRTEEN

His quarters were a mess. Nothing was destroyed, but everything was out of place and there were empty spaces where his equipment had been. They'd gone through everything, even his drawers and closets. He made sure the door was closed and locked behind him before he went to the desk and crouched behind it. The hiding spot he'd built into it was still closed, and he breathed a sigh of relief. At least one thing had gone right today.

He retrieved the device and plugged it into his data port. For the next five minutes he roamed his quarters as he tried to connect with Nyx, but nothing got through. She must have temporarily shut down the channel.

Veth. How could he help if she wouldn't even speak to him? He didn't even know where she was… but there might be a way he could find out. He'd need access to a computer system, and they hadn't left so much as a broken circuit board in his quarters. His best bet was the *Malora*. The general had ordered his quarters searched, but no one had mentioned the ship.

He grabbed his go-bag - the one item in his place that had been carefully repacked after being searched – double-checked the contents, and set out for the far side of the station where the *Malora* was docked.

He had time to think on the way over, running through the most likely scenarios. The odds were good that if she thought she was being hunted, she'd try to get off the station. But how? She didn't have ID or scrip to buy her way off, which left stowing away or stealing a ship.

He checked the *Malora's* security log the second he set foot on her deck. It showed that no one had been onboard since yesterday. *Good.*

After that, it was simply a matter of cobbling together a few bits of spare tech he had lying around his cramped workspace and figuring out how to connect the various devices to the ship's navigational system. Then all he had to do was ping her location. It had a limited range, but she couldn't have gotten far. Even if she'd found a way off the station, all ships were required to use standard engines until they reached a safe minimum distance from the Drift. FTL Drives were just too dangerous when there were so many ships and other objects floating around local space.

He set everything up, stared at the jumble of parts he'd thrown together, and briefly questioned his life choices as he plugged himself into his makeshift matrix and hoped he'd got everything right. "Here goes nothing."

He didn't go all the way into cyberspace this time. Instead of stepping into the digital realm, it was as if part of the realm flowed out into reality. He was still in his chair and could still smell the unique perfume of circuitry, metal, and ozone that filled his little corner of the ship, but he could see data flowing around him, and hear the subtle buzz of the datasphere.

He sent the ping, and whooped in triumph when he got an immediate fix on her position. His jubilation was short-lived, though. She wasn't on Astek anymore. He sent several more pings in quick succession, getting a reading on her course and relative speed. She was heading into the asteroid field, which made no sense, but she was moving slowly enough he'd be able to catch her. If he could find a ship.

He unplugged from the system, packed the equipment into his bag, and got to his feet, already running through a list of people he could call on for help. The cyborgs who ran the Nova Club would step up to protect one of their own, or he had a favor or two he could call in from some of the freight pilots that came and went from the Drift. He couldn't take the *Malora*—the moment he released the docking clamps they'd know she was in flight and come after him. He couldn't ask for permission to go after her, either. If Halverson learned where she was or that she was trackable, he'd toss Eric in a cell and send someone else after her. That wouldn't end well for anyone, because his beautiful, dangerous starshine wouldn't go down easily.

No, he had to do this quietly, and he had to do this alone. This wasn't about fixing things with Nyx anymore. This was about making sure she got a chance to live the life the Gray Men had stolen from her, whether he was a part of it or not.

He was already composing the message he'd send to Dax after he was gone, taking full responsibility for his actions. Even if nothing else stuck, going AWOL and disobeying orders to stay on the station would cost him, but if he had to trade his future for Nyx's, that was a price he was happy to pay.

"This is not Rossi's office, Erben," Kurt's voice came over the ship's speakers.

"Oh, come on!" he muttered.

"Get your ass to the briefing room, Ensign. Since you failed to come to us, we came to you. Double time!" Kurt barked.

"Yessir, on my way!" He broke into a run and made it to the briefing room in a matter of seconds. Whatever came next, there was no point in delaying it.

The door slid open at a touch and he walked inside, expecting to be met by the disapproving stares of his XO and commander. Instead, the entire team was seated around the table, all of them grinning at him but Dax, who stood much as he had earlier, arms folded, jaw set, eyes narrowed.

"Care to explain why you didn't follow Sabre's very

simple instructions?" Dax asked, every word cool and clipped.

Eric came to attention. "I needed to find Nyx, sir."

"And did you?"

He hesitated for a moment, but the only people in the entire galaxy he trusted with the truth were all in this room. If he couldn't help Nyx, maybe they could. "I did. She's not on the station any longer. She's running."

Dante cursed, and Aria leaned forward in her chair, fingers steepled in front of her. "Where's she headed?"

"Into the asteroid field," Eric said.

"Why would she go that way?" Cris asked.

"I don't know. She's not answering me."

Dax's lips twitched in what might have been a smile or a grimace. "And how would she be able to do that when your comm unit was seized to prevent you from contacting her?"

The way this day was going he was going to have to start inventing new curse words, because muttering *fraxx* every few minutes was really getting old. "I had another means of communication, sir."

Dante snickered, and Trinity hid her face behind an upraised hand.

"Of course you did. Did you have this when you were in my office?"

"No sir. It was in my quarters."

"And yet, it wasn't seized with the rest of your things?" Dax asked.

"It was. Uh. It was in a hard to find location."

The room broke out in snickers and soft guffaws of

laughter, and even Dax smiled a little. "You're a pain in my ass, Erben. You realize that?"

"You've mentioned it once or twice, sir."

Dax sat down, looking more relaxed now, and gestured for Eric to do the same. "You were going after her, weren't you?"

"I was. I have to."

"And you weren't going to ask us to help, because you wanted to keep us out of trouble, right?" Kurt asked, his voice tight with frustration.

"Yeah."

Kurt grunted and slapped a hand on the table. "I'm done with this deniability crap. You took the blame for breaking the rules and going into cyberspace to track down Project Fury, even though I'm the one who told you to pursue it."

Dax stared at his XO. "You did what? Dammit, Sabre, I leave you in charge one time…"

Sabre looked around the table, then at Dax. "And when you came back from your well-deserved time off, we had a lead to follow. Finally. We're fighting a war against an enemy with no limits. If we don't step over the line from time to time, we're going to lose."

Everyone was quiet for a long moment.

Finally, Dante nodded. "Sabre's right. I'm not saying we need to go rogue, but if we play it straight, we're going to get our heads handed to us."

"And our asses," Aria chimed in.

"They tried to kill my sister. They've tried to kill

members of this team. We need a new game plan," Cris agreed.

"Meyer only knew what I'd done after I'd already done it. The choice was mine. I was tired of hitting dead ends because I had to follow the rules," Eric stated.

"I see." Dax sat back in his chair and looked around the table. "Anyone else feel this way?"

Trinity leaned in. "You know my feelings already."

Dax rapped his knuckles on the table. "Alright then. It's unanimous. Not that this is a democracy by any means, but I needed to know where everyone stood. It's time we changed playbooks."

There was a murmur of approval and anticipation from around the table, but all Eric felt was gratitude for his team.

"So, what's the plan?" Aria asked.

Dax cocked his brow and nodded to Eric. "Good question. Magi, what's our plan?"

Eric stood up. "We take the *Malora* and find Nyx before anyone else does. Someone wants her isolated and vulnerable, and we're the only ones in a position to make sure that doesn't happen. I have her basic course and speed, it won't take us long to catch up to her. I'll relay the information to the onboard nav-system once we're done here."

"Any idea what ship she's on?"

"None, though given where she's headed, it's not likely to be a freighter or a passenger ship. She's probably liberated a mining vessel. Blink, would you please find out if any ships have been reported missing or stolen in the past hour or so?"

"You got it," Aria said.

"There's one more thing I need to tell you. You're all aware that Nyx has a minor psychic link to her clones. What she didn't tell you was that there's still a fury out there, and the last time Nyx had contact with her she was with Absalom – or more accurately, she's with his younger clone. Nyx hasn't had contact since we rescued her, but if that fury is still alive out there, she's our best chance of finding Absalom's clone and shutting him down for good."

"Why are we only just learning this now?" Dax asked.

"I didn't know until a few days ago, and Nyx was afraid that if the information got out, she'd be subjected to more tests. I was trying to convince her that wouldn't happen, but after today's events, it's clear she was right to be worried. If Halverson found out…" He didn't finish the sentence. He didn't have to.

Aria chimed in without looking up from her data tablet. "She's on the "Double Jeopardy." It was due for an overhaul, but the owner hasn't come up with the down payment yet. The ship was unguarded and sitting in a side hangar. The report just came in. It's a mining vessel, slow, well armored, minimal weaponry. Slower still since it's got just one working engine."

"We'll get her back, Magi." Dante rose and started for the door. "Send the navigational data. I'm going to warm up the engines and prep for takeoff. Sir, what should I say is our reason for this unscheduled departure?"

Eric spoke up. "That's easy. Tell them we're recovering stolen property."

Dax nodded. "Works for me."

And with that, the meeting ended and everyone headed to their stations. Eric smiled as he went with them. Things were finally starting to go his way. Now he just had to hope that whatever Nyx was planning, she wouldn't start until after they'd caught up to her.

LEAVING HURT MORE than she could have imagined. In all the years she'd planned her revenge, she'd never considered that she might have anything, or anyone, to leave behind. She'd existed all that time without friends, a home, or someone she cared about. But now she had those things, or at least she had the potential for them. Eric might care about her because she reminded him of someone else, but he did care for her.

His teammates were kind, and getting to know Tyra had given her insight into what it might be like to have friends. She'd miss other things, too. Simple ones, like ice cream and hot showers, the comforting warmth of falling asleep in someone's arms. She'd been foolish to let herself be distracted by those things, but she couldn't bring herself to regret it. At least she'd gotten a taste of what life might have been like. It would have to be enough.

Her anger at Eric had faded a little. His words hurt, but how could she be angry at him for not remembering who she was when she was having trouble figuring it out for herself? She was a mixed-up mess of other people's memories and experiences. The only thing she was certain of right now was her mission. She needed to get to Absalom. That was *her* goal, no one else's.

Eric had let her hear Echo's final message to him. At the time, she thought she'd understood her clone's last words, but she hadn't really, not until now. Echo had said that what she'd shared with Eric had never been meant to be, and that she was dead before they'd even met. Now, she got it.

As Nyx piloted the partially crippled ship she'd stolen farther away from the station and everyone she cared about, she allowed herself to shed a handful of tears for the life she'd never get to have. One way or another, she would end Project Fury. If she didn't die in the attempt, then she'd end up locked away again, at least until she found a way to end her life and escape once and for all. Echo had been wrong about one thing – Eric couldn't save her. Not from this. This had always been her destiny.

Once she was certain she'd gotten away without being noticed, she activated the ship's autopilot and went looking for something she could use to help her keep warm. She'd rerouted power from every system to the ship's single engine, and with only minimal life support and no environmental controls, the temperature was dropping fast. Her nanotech would protect her from any serious harm, but between the cold and the thinner atmosphere, it wouldn't be a comfortable journey.

She didn't find much on board, but her feet were now clad in an extra pair of socks, and she'd commandeered the blankets from the crew's quarters and made a comfy nest for herself in the cockpit. The ship's rudimentary AI could maintain course and heading, but her makeshift repairs and overrides were more than it could comprehend. She'd have to stay close and make manual adjustments as needed or she'd never reach her destination.

At least she'd have time to come up with a plan. She'd chosen the ship as much for its appearance as it's availability. The *Double Jeopardy* was a mining vessel and wouldn't look out of place where she was going. Her best bet was to limp into sensor range while broadcasting a distress signal. The ship she'd stolen still had mining equipment on board, including several laser drills and a surprising quantity of explosives. She had the means to take her revenge. She just needed to get herself onboard and find a way to free her clone. That way at least one of them would get the chance to live, to experience everything she'd only gotten a taste of.

By the time she spotted the incoming ship, it had almost overtaken her. Despite her routing precious power to the sensors to monitor the area, there'd been no alerts and no sign of any other traffic until the *Malora* was suddenly coming up on her port side. *How the* fraxx *did he find me?*

The comms signaled an incoming message. She stared at it for a long time before finally giving in to the inevitable and opened a channel, voice only. "I'm not going back."

"I guessed that much, but you're not going to get very far in that derelict, either. It's been reported stolen already." Eric's voice came over the line, wrapping around her soul like a warm, soft blanket she wanted to curl into.

She stiffened her spine and pushed the thought away. She couldn't let herself get distracted again. "They won't be able to find me. The transponder met with an unfortunate accident."

Someone in the background sniggered softly. "I wonder where she learned that expression."

"You're not helping, Buttercup," Eric said, his voice slightly muffled as if his head was turned away. Then in a clearer voice he added. "Do you even know who you're running from?"

"The ones who arrested you." She paused then added. "I take it the charges didn't stick?"

"They weren't supposed to. They were just supposed to get me taken out of play. I don't think I was ever the real target. You were, and you're not going to be able to fend them off by yourself. I know you're pissed at me, and you've got a good reason, but please, let us help."

"No." She didn't want him around for this. It was

her mission, and she didn't want to drag anyone else into it. He couldn't get hurt if he wasn't involved.

"Nyx. We're not sure who is behind this, or what their endgame is. You're out here in a crippled ship with next to no weapons, and … *Re'veth*. Why is your life support shut off?"

"I re-routed the power. Quit being so nosy and go back to Astek. You worry about saving your own ass. I'll take care of mine."

"I don't want to leave you out here on your own. Friends don't do that."

"We're not friends." It wasn't true. He was the only real friend she'd ever had, which was why he was the only one with the power to hurt her. She needed to finish her mission, but he didn't have to go with her. He was safer without her around.

"The hell we're not. I'm here because I care about you. You, Nyx. Not Echo or any other woman in the galaxy. Just you."

"Stop. We're not talking about this. Not now." She couldn't have this conversation. "Eric, you need to listen to me. I can do this on my own. In fact, it's better this way. If you're right, they went after you to get to me. I made you a target. Let me go and finish this. My way."

"Hold on a second, I'm encrypting this connection."

She pursed her lips. "You don't have to do that."

"Yeah, I think I do. Okay, we're secure now. So, tell me I'm wrong. Tell me you're not going after Absalom and your clone alone."

She didn't say anything.

Eric sighed. "That's what I thought."

"And now your teammates know, which means they'll never let me do this alone. You agreed not to say anything."

"I agreed not to say anything until there was actionable intel. I'd say this qualifies. But if you really want to do this alone, no one here is going to stop you."

That surprised her. "No?"

"No. But you've got a snowball's chance in a supernova of pulling this off if you don't have help."

"I'll manage."

"How?"

She gave in and activated the visual just so she could glare at him. His face appeared on one of the monitors in the console, his dark eyes locked on hers with an intensity that made her hard retort turn to dust in her mouth. He was worried about her. *He cared.*

"Hey, starshine. It's good to see your face."

"I didn't open the line to get compliments. I needed to see you so I could make you understand that I'm serious. I don't want anyone coming with me."

"Why not?" he pressed.

Because she wasn't planning on coming back from this, and she didn't want to take anyone else with her. Probably not the answer that would get him to back off, but it was the truth. "Because you're in enough trouble already."

"The way I see it, that's the argument I should be

making to you, not the other way around. The best way to get us both out of trouble is to find Absalom and retrieve as much data as we can about the Grays. That's ample proof we're not working for him, or anyone else."

Dax stepped into view behind Eric's shoulder and nodded in greeting. "Magi's right. If we go in together, we've got a better chance of succeeding."

And if she had help, her clone's chances of survival increased significantly. *Fraxx*. "If I agree to this, I want your word that someone finds my clone and escorts her back to the *Malora*."

"Agreed. We'll make sure she makes it out," Dax said.

"Thank you, Commander."

Eric's expression hadn't changed. "Does this mean you're coming aboard?"

"We're going in together. All of us. No one will get in my way?" she asked. She'd need to move fast to get close enough to Absalom to finish him before he could shut her down. The others could create enough of a distraction to make that happen.

"Together," Eric agreed.

"I'm only doing this because it means a better chance of success. I won't let him get away again."

A flash of understanding and something deeper gleamed in Eric's eyes. "I know."

"Okay, then. I guess I'm coming aboard. Any thoughts on what to do with the *Jeopardy*?"

"We'll put an evidence tag on it. That should keep

anyone from trying to tow or salvage it until we get back – where are we going, anyway?" Dax asked.

"About a day and a half journey from here."

"Son of a *fraxxing* starbeast. He's *here*? This close?"

"Arrogant bastard,"

"Cocky son of a—"

"He's taunting us."

Only Eric stayed quiet. When the outburst was over, he touched a hand to his chest, right over his heart. "We'll get him, Nyx."

She didn't bother correcting him. There was no we. She'd be going after Absalom alone, and she had no intention of bringing him back alive.

CHAPTER FOURTEEN

ERIC WAS in the main briefing room, preparing for one last run-through before they arrived. He'd rather have been with Nyx, but she'd been keeping her distance since he'd met her at the airlock door and welcomed her on board.

It wasn't the reunion he'd been hoping for, but at least she was on the *Malora*. Dax had reported the situation to Colonel Bahl, and she'd granted permission to proceed with the mission while she engaged in some high-level maneuvering to protect the team and minimize the fallout when General Halverson realized what was going on.

The ship was in stealth mode, and Dante was making the best speed he could while making his way through the unchartable and ever-changing field of asteroids outside. The big stuff was easy to avoid, but the deeper they went, the denser the debris became.

Between random collisions and intentional demolitions, this area was full of smaller chunks of rock and the remains of a few unlucky mining vessels.

He felt like he was piloting his own private asteroid field at the moment. Nyx was withdrawn and he didn't know how to reach her. Every time he got too close, she retreated behind a barrage of questions about their attack plan, and he hadn't been able to sidestep her queries fast enough to talk to her about anything else.

They were already within sensor range, and so far, there'd been no reaction from the target. As advanced as the Gray's tech was, he'd been worried Absalom would detect them despite the *Malora's* stealth ability, but it didn't appear that was the case. The *Malora* would be able to get in close before they had to reveal themselves, which was a good thing. Based on what he'd gleaned by scanning hundreds of reports by miners in the area, Absalom wasn't on a station. They were going after another ship, which meant they'd have to cripple their opponent's engines the moment they dropped out of stealth mode or risk losing their target in the asteroid field.

There were less than a dozen sightings of the ship they were after, but it was enough to scrape together a description. He'd run the details through every database he could legally access and come up with two matches. They were both variations on a single model, and their blueprints were close enough he'd been able to figure out a plan.

He'd taken it to Nyx next. That had been the longest

conversation they'd had. Her input had been invaluable, and between them they'd come up with a workable approach that had impressed Dax when they'd brought it to him for approval. There was only one problem with it. Nyx had resisted every attempt he'd made to partner her with anyone. She was determined to do this on her own, and he didn't like it. She might have come back to the *Malora*, but she hadn't stopped running.

He drummed his fingers on the tabletop in frustration, the noise seeming louder in the otherwise silent room. What was she running from, though? The obvious answer was him, but he didn't think that was the whole story, and he was almost out of time to figure it out.

He'd left the door open, and Trinity walked in. "You okay? You look like someone increased the gravity in here by a factor of three."

"All good. Just going through the plan."

She dropped into the seat across from him. "Fido said it's solid, which is high praise coming from him." Her voice lowered. "So, what are you really thinking about? Or can I guess?"

"If you're asking, you already know the answer."

"Still mad at you?"

"She's got good reason to be."

"I take it you've apologized?"

He shot her an annoyed look and she held up her hands. "Right. Of course you did."

"Several times. She's not interested in talking about it. She's all about the mission right now."

"And afterward?" Trin asked, keeping her voice down so it wouldn't carry outside the room.

"I don't know. I get the feeling she doesn't expect there to be an afterward. Not for her."

Trin's amber eyes widened. "Well, that's not good. You sure?"

"Honestly? No. It's just a gut feeling."

She leaned in. "Have you told her how you feel?"

He barked out a laugh. "When would I have managed that? The only thing she wants to hear from me is battle plans. Anything else and she's out of the room like a streaking comet. Do you know how fast cyborgs can move when they want to? I blink, she's gone."

"If you get a chance to tell her, take it. Don't wait for the perfect moment." She gave him a small smile. "I was angry at Dax for a long time. It was easier to focus on my goals if I could blame him for what happened to my brother. Anger's a damned good motivator. It kept me going for years."

"So why did you stop being angry at him?"

"Because he told me the truth about what happened to Travis."

He spread his hands out, palms up. "That doesn't help me, Trin. I don't have any secrets to tell."

"Yes, you do. Tell her, Eric. I got a second chance to work things out with Dax. Not everyone gets that lucky." She leaned back in her chair as more footsteps sounded in the corridor outside. The team was arriving. It was time to get to work. He'd find a way to talk to Nyx before they arrived at their destination. Trin was right. If he didn't, he might not get another chance.

Nyx had been avoiding Eric since coming aboard, but he'd found ways to talk to her, anyway. She had to be on her guard or he would have found a way to slip under her defenses again, and part of her wanted that too much to let it happen.

She was on her way to their last briefing, her thoughts racing around her head fuelled by adrenaline and anticipation. This was it. Her moment was coming. Eric had even come to her with the blueprints and his preliminary plan. He'd included her despite the fact he was worried about her.

She bounced her fist against her side as she walked, the plan fading away as thoughts of Eric filled her head. The lunatic had risked everything to come after her. They all had, a fact that gratified and humbled her. She'd expected him to push her, use the fact he'd risked his future for her to get her to talk to him, but he hadn't brought it up. She'd learned the details of Eric's situation from Trinity over a meal in the mess.

He'd shown up when she needed him and folded her back into the team as if she hadn't run. She'd be lying to herself if she pretended it didn't mean anything. He was a good man. Imperfect and reckless, but his heart was kind. Now they were at the end of their time together, she could see that. Maybe he'd be the one to find the last fury. He could take care of her, help her build a new life, maybe one with him…

Her heart twisted and every part of her screamed in denial at the thought. It didn't matter that the fury was her clone. It wouldn't be *her* with Eric. It would be someone else. A stranger neither of them had ever met. The reality hit her like a comet strike, obliterating the idea that she and her clones were interchangeable beings. They weren't. *She* was an individual. One with a rotten sense of *fraxxing* timing. Her revelation changed everything, and nothing. Individual or not, she was still a cyborg, and she had a mission to finish. Nothing else mattered.

She squared her shoulders and hurried to the briefing room.

She filed in behind Cris and Aria, who were exchanging insults as they walked, though there was no anger behind the words. If Eric was right about the two of them, they had the oddest way of showing their affection for each other.

Eric was seated in his usual spot and the ship's three-dimensional schematics were projected over the table in a slowly rotating display. Everyone took their seats quickly, and somehow, she wound up sitting beside him.

The talk died away the moment Dax rapped his knuckles on the tabletop. "This is our last run-through. Remember, no plan survives contact with the enemy, and this one is going to be particularly fluid because we've got minimal intel to work off. We'll go around the table and I want each of you to state your primary and secondary objectives, starting with Strak, who is listening in from the cockpit."

"I'm babysitting the *fraxxing* ship. Again," the big Torski's voice rumbled from the room's speakers. "Secondary objective is to track you lot as you make your way to your targets and report the location of anyone on the other team."

"Next time, I'll pilot and you shoot things," Eric said, a smile playing on his handsome face. Her heart warmed at that small smile, and a quiet voice whispered to her that if she wanted to see it again all she had to do was reach out and take his hand.

"Rossi, do not let that lunatic near my ship's controls. Ever," Dante punctuated his statement with a growl.

Dax just rolled his eyes. "Can we get on with the briefing, now?"

"Sorry, sir." Both Eric and Dante spoke at the same time, and she ducked her head to hide her amusement.

"Thank you." Rossi pointed to himself. "I'm going to the bridge to take control of the vessel and subdue anyone I find on the way there. Once there, I hold the location and attempt to assist the rest of you by unlocking doors, altering gravity, taking over automated defense systems, and anything else I can manage."

Trinity spoke up next. "I'm with Rossi. Same objectives."

"And I'm with his lordship and Sabre. We're to do a level by level sweep looking for captives, priority given to locating Nyx's last clone," Aria said. "Secondary missions are to subdue anyone not in this room and mark any labs for further investigation once the ship is secure."

Nyx nodded in gratitude. This time they'd be looking for any genetic material Absalom might have onboard, including maturation tanks and cloning labs. Anything they found would be identified and eventually destroyed. Dax had given her his word.

"I'm with Jessop. Same objectives. It's my job to identify medical areas while Blink shoots the bad guys like the badass that she is."

Aria snorted in amusement. "And don't you forget it."

"And I'm going with Caldwell and Jessop in case someone gets hurt and Caldwell has to switch to medic mode and split off to treat one of the team," Kurt stated.

Eric spoke up next. "My primary goal is to take down the ship's defense systems, shut down any system wipes, and start the transfer of data to the *Malora*." He stopped, then turned to face Nyx. "Then, I'm going to accompany Nyx when she goes off on whatever insane plan she has to find Absalom and take him down."

She stared at him. That was not the plan they'd agreed on. She was supposed to be disabling the escape pods and shuttle bays, which was where she thought she had the best chance of finding Absalom when he tried to flee. "That's not the plan."

"I'm changing the plan." Eric took her hand in his and squeezed. "Did you really think I was going to let you do this alone, starshine?"

"This isn't your mission."

He stood and pulled her into his arms. She could have resisted, but she didn't want to. If this was their last moment, then she wanted to feel him hold her one more time.

"You need to understand something. Your mission might be to find Absalom and make sure he pays for what he's done, but I have my own mission." He leaned in and brushed a tender kiss to her mouth, letting his lips glide over hers and sending tingles all the way down to her toes. "In case you haven't figured it out, yet. My mission, is you. I know who you are, Nyx. You're the only woman I care about, never doubt it."

She should have pushed him away, or turned her head, or said something to stop him, but instead she twined her arms around his neck and kissed him back. He groaned deep in his chest, one arm coming around her back to hold her close, the other cupping the back of her head. They came together perfectly, two halves of a whole she'd been denying existed. His mouth was a brand against her skin, and as his tongue tangled with hers she could taste a hint of cocoa and whipped cream. For her, it was the best flavor in the galaxy, because it reminded her of him.

Heat poured into her, and something deep inside her chest cracked open.

She held him tight as hope, bright and beautiful, welled up inside her. She wanted him. More than she'd wanted anything else in her entire life, she wanted this, and she couldn't have it.

He whispered her name against her lips with a reverence that made her heart soar. "I love you. Whatever happens next, whatever choice you make, I needed you to know that."

She shivered, eyes closing to hide the tears that burned her eyes. He loved her. She didn't doubt his words for a moment. How could she? But she couldn't answer him, either. There wasn't time for all the things she wanted to say, so she kissed him, slow and sweet this time, letting him taste her tears as they fell.

It was all she could give him.

"About damned time," Cris muttered.

There was a muffled sound of someone being kicked with a combat boot, followed by a grunt. "Hey! What was that for," Cris demanded?

"Ruining the moment. Seriously, Trip, don't you have any romance in your soul?" Aria asked.

"I did. Then someone I know told me to toss it out an air—" There was another thump, louder this time, and Cris stopped talking mid-sentence.

Nyx pulled back, knowing their moment was over, but Eric didn't let go of her. Instead, he gently brushed the tears from her cheeks, then kissed her one last time.

"This conversation isn't over. It's just on hold," he told her.

"Until later," she agreed.

"Later." There was a wealth of promise in that single word, and it made her heart ache to know there wasn't much chance she'd ever be able to collect on that promise.

CHAPTER FIFTEEN

ERIC WAS STRUCK by a powerful sense of deja-vu as they all stood, geared up and ready to go after the Gray Men, all waiting on Dante's signal.

It wasn't exactly the same, though. This time he wouldn't have to search for Nyx. He'd be right behind her, watching her back as she went up against the man who'd held her prisoner for years. He glanced over at Nyx, who was standing beside him in serene silence, one hand resting lightly on the grip of the blaster Dax had provided from the ship's stores. She was wearing borrowed body armor, the black, form-fitting pieces making her look hotter than a supernova. She looked good in anything, and nothing at all, but he liked her best when she looked like this: dangerous and ready to wreak havoc.

She was holding the bulkhead with her other hand, and he shifted his grip so that he could hold the same one. He wanted to be close to her. Hell, he didn't plan on letting her out of his sight, because he still couldn't shake the feeling she didn't plan on coming back from this mission.

"Dropping out of stealth mode in three, two, one, mark." Dante announced. Incoming fire slammed against their shields only a few seconds later, and they all braced their feet as the ship reacted to the impact. They had to be using kinetic missiles to make the ship shudder and rock that way.

"Well, they seem friendly," Aria quipped.

There was a riff of tight laughter but it didn't change the level of anticipation in the air.

"What's going on, Strak?" Dax asked.

"Their shields were stronger than anticipated, but I got through. They're crippled. I'm taking out their weapons at the moment. These guys have military-grade defenses, sir. Impressive ones."

Another shudder rocked the ship, though it was significantly less powerful than the previous barrage.

"Damage report?" Dax asked Eric. He turned and scanned a display on the wall behind him. "Shields holding at seventy-six percent. No damage."

"Strak?"

"Target has been immobilized and defenses destroyed. I'm bringing us in. The primary boarding location is a go. Contact in less than ninety seconds."

There was a collective intake of breath as they prepared for the next stage. Dante had done his part, now it was up to them. Eric looked around, meeting his friend's faces and reading the determination in their eyes. They were here because of him. They'd risked their careers because they believed in him, and now they were risking their lives following a plan he'd come up with. He cleared his throat and everyone turned to look at him. "I just wanted to say thank you. None of you had to come with me, but you showed up anyway. You're the best team, and the best friends, in the *fraxxing* galaxy. So, thank you."

"Aw man! Magi's getting sappy and I'm not there to see his face. This is not fair, Rossi," Dante grumbled.

"I love you too, my friend. I'll come give you a big squishy hug later," Eric called, grinning.

"Smartass. Hang on, we're about to make contact. This is going to get a little…*Fraxx*! Brace-Brace-Brace!"

Eric barely had time to register Dante's warning before the ship lurched and an ear-piercing screech of twisting metal tore through the air.

"Sonofabitch used their thrusters to swing into us at the last minute!"

"Damage report!" Dax demanded.

Eric scanned the readout. "Extensive external damage. One breach in sector two-dash-eight, directly below us. Repair droids deployed, automated systems responding."

"It was a glancing blow. I managed to rotate the ship enough to avoid a direct hit. Sneaky *vething* bastards. Be careful in there. This isn't going to be like the last mission."

Dax looked grim. "You heard the man. Don't get cocky."

"Cocky gets you dead," they recited in unison. It was an old IAF expression taught to every soldier during basic training.

Eric looked at Nyx in surprise. She'd recited it along with the others. "Where'd you learn that?"

She tapped her temple. "The corporations didn't have time to send their war toys to basic training, so they implanted what we needed to know. I guess that was part of the programming I received."

"You did basic training while you were asleep?" Cris sounded envious. "Damn, and I had to do it the hard way."

There wasn't time for anyone to respond to Cris' comment before they linked to the other ship and started the boarding sequence. This time, they stayed well clear of the door as the bulkhead fell.

"Two life signs taking position twenty meters away from our entry point and more on the way," Dante warned.

Cris slapped a button on the panel, and a temporary shield shimmered into existence over the doorway just in time to absorb the incoming barrage of blaster bolts fired at them. The energy bolts sizzled against the shield while Trinity and Aria took up positions on either side of the door. They took their time lining up their shots through the blaze of incoming fire, but they both dropped their targets on the first shot.

The shield dropped, and they stormed onto the

Enigma, everyone peeling off in pairs and heading off to their assigned tasks. Eric palmed the data stick he'd liberated from his stash of 'not-exactly-legal' tech onboard the *Malora* and looked for the nearest data node or access panel. This was the part of the plan Nyx hadn't known about. The data stick was full of copies of his digital sprites, programmed to self-replicate, spread out, copy whatever data they could, and return to the ship's system as soon as their task was done. He was going to break a string of laws and protocols, but it was the only way they could be sure they got what they needed to win the battle against the Grays.

He sprinted down a hallway, trusting Nyx to deal with anyone who tried to stop them. Blaster fire streaked past him, and an automated gun exploded into sparks and shrapnel before he made it halfway to his goal. "Nice shot!"

"You're insane!" She called back. "Next time, give me a second to clear the area before you start running."

"I knew you had my back."

She caught up a few strides before he reached the console he'd spotted earlier. "How long will it take you to get what you need?"

"Not long." He placed a hand on the console, turned, and leaned in to steal a kiss. He'd intended it to be brief, but when she opened her mouth and wrapped her arm around his waist, he forgot about everything else for a few perfect, blissful moments. He breathed in the scent of her, memorizing the soft play of her lips as they moved under his.

They broke away from each other at the same moment, both of them breathing harder than they had been a few seconds before. "Hold that thought. And for the record, you are *fraxxing* sexy in combat gear. See you soon, starshine."

This was the part of the plan Dax hadn't liked. Eric needed to jack into the system briefly to shut down the automated defenses and make sure there were no surprises waiting for them. It would also give them a good shot at locating Absalom and Nyx's clone, but it came with risks. While he was jacked-in, he was vulnerable. Eric trusted Nyx not to go after Absalom alone, leaving him unguarded, but Dax had reservations. In the end, he'd let Eric make the call.

She set her hand on his shoulder. "Do it."

He plugged in and crossed into another world. He had a job to do, and the sooner he got it done, the sooner he and Nyx could move on to their next objective – payback.

FOR NYX, every second he was gone felt like an eternity. Part of her was screaming that she could leave him here and go after Absalom alone. He'd be safe enough, and every second she waited her quarry was getting further away. But he trusted her to watch his back, and she would not betray that trust.

She tightened her hand on his shoulder as she scanned for any sign of danger. He was so still it was eerie, his body emptied of all animation so it was like holding onto a mannequin. She missed his smile, his laugh, the way his mouth ticked up at one corner when he was amused. He had more life and energy than anyone else she'd met, and it didn't feel right to see him like this, silent and still.

Without thinking, she brushed a kiss to his ear and whispered, "Come back to me, lover."

He shivered, inhaled sharply and straightened up. Without a word he turned and kissed her, pressing her up against the wall of the corridor with a suddenness that took her breath away.

"What was that for?" she asked when he finally raised his head again.

"Staying with me, *lover*," he stressed the last word, and she realized he must have heard her calling to him.

An unfamiliar heat warmed her cheeks and her throat tightened a little, but there wasn't time for that now. They needed to go. "Did you find him?"

"You were right. Shuttle bay one. Main level." He relayed that information to the others over their comms.

"Moving the *Malora* to that side of the station," Dante reported, and cursed a few seconds later. "*Fraxx*. There's a shuttle breaking away on the far side. Which one do I focus on, Commander?"

"Absalom is our main target. Stay on your current course. You got missile lock?"

"Already firing, sir, but the shuttle is evading. Dammit, the *Enigma* is blocking my direct line of sight so I can't use the cannons."

Nyx pushed thoughts of the other shuttle out of her head. They didn't matter. Only Absalom did, and he was in shuttle bay one, which was on the same level they were. She had memorized the ship's layout and knew exactly where to go. She was going to get her shot. A thought occurred to her and she took Eric's hand, pulling his attention back to her.

"If something happens to me, promise me you'll finish this."

Eric shook his head sharply. "Nothing is going to happen to you."

"Promise me!" She'd always expected to do this alone, but now she realized this was better. No matter what happened to her, the team would see justice done. It wouldn't be as satisfying as the revenge she had planned, but it would be enough. If she didn't die in vain, it would be enough.

"I promise." He narrowed his eyes. "What do you think is going to happen? Why do I keep feeling that this is goodbye?"

She shook her head. There wasn't time to explain. "Later."

He stepped back and drew his blaster. "Just make sure there is a later. You hear me?"

She smiled as a ribbon of almost manic joy wound its way around her heart. One way or another, she was going to keep her promise to the others. "I hear you, love." She was off and running before he had time to react, but she heard him laughing as he followed her down the corridor. She might be running toward her death, but she wasn't running alone, and that made all the difference.

She was almost to the shuttle bay doors when Absalom's cold, polished voice came over the ship's speakers. "Hello again, Subject One. I wondered if you were part of this ill-conceived attack. I'm glad you came, because it gives me a chance to say something I couldn't last time." He paused for half a heartbeat before speaking again. "Goodbye, Subject One."

No! She skidded to a stop as fear gripped her in a strangle hold, crushing her ribs and making it almost impossible to breathe. She'd never considered… never thought about… dammit! She turned to Eric and held out her hand to him, knowing she only had a second or two left.

"I lov—" She didn't get to finish speaking before Absalom spoke one of the nonsensical phrases she'd learned to dread, the shutdown command she couldn't override.

She waited for the inevitable spike of pain that came before the darkness swept over her…but nothing happened. She didn't know whether to scream in defiance or sob with relief. It hadn't worked! Laughter burst out of her, giving voice to her feelings in a long, joyful exhalation that rang off the walls of the corridor.

Eric stared at her, elated and somewhat confused. He raised his head and called out to the air. "Hey asshole, don't interrupt my lady when she's talking." Then he winked at her. "I'm not sure what's going on, but before you explain, can you say that again, starshine?"

She threw herself into his arms, still bouncing with relief and euphoria. "I love you, you lunatic. But I don't understand. I should be unconscious, or dead." Absalom had told her more than once he could kill her with a word if he wished. She thought he'd do it… but he hadn't. Or couldn't.

"So, you learned how to deactivate the code. Disappointing." Absalom sounded almost bored, but she knew him well enough to detect the undertone of annoyance in his words. He didn't like it when things didn't go according to plan.

She threw out the challenge she'd held close to her heart for so long. "I'm coming for you, Absalom. Do you hear me? You're going to pay for what you did to me and the furies. You're going to pay for all of it!"

There was no response. Not that she expected one. Absalom was too smart to linger now that the odds weren't in his favor.

"Come on!" She sprinted toward the shuttle bay, leaving Eric behind after only a few strides. She needed to reach Absalom before he got away. She might never find him again.

"Nyx, you copy?" It was Aria.

She cursed and slowed enough to tap her comms, leaving the channel open for two-way communication. "This is Nyx."

"We need you on the medical levels. Hurry."

She wanted to refuse, but something in Aria's tone made her hesitate. "Why?"

"It's the fury. Some bitch ordered her to attack us. I had to...She's dying. Cris says he can't save her, but you might be able to. Something about your nanotech being compatible?"

Medi-bots were genetically coded, and the fury was her clone. If she was bleeding out, she'd be losing medi-bots too fast for them to heal her, but if the clone got a fresh infusion she might live. *Might*.

Nyx beat her fist against her thigh in frustration. Eric stood in front of her, steady and silent, waiting for her to make her choice. A sudden flood of cool gratitude poured over the fire of her fury, cooling it. Eric was with her. She didn't *have* to choose.

She grabbed him by the front of his uniform and hauled him in for a quick kiss. "Kick his ass for me, lover."

Then she was off again, flying down the corridor as she recalled the route to the medical decks. "Blink, it's Nyx. I'm on my way."

The layout of the ship was remarkably similar to the last station she'd been held on, and part of her brain wondered if they'd been designed by the same person, or at least at the same facility. She bypassed the elevator in favor of the ladders that linked the floors, jumping from level to level in a matter of seconds.

She listened to the battle chatter as she ran, not that there was much actual combat going on. Trinity and Dax had taken over the bridge, and judging by the carnage on the medical level, Cris and Aria had eliminated all the resistance in the area.

She ran past a half-dozen dead bodies, all of them armed and wearing security patches on their arms. She scanned them as she passed, looking for anyone familiar. She found two faces she recognized, and was startled to see them on more than one of the bodies. Clones. Eric had been right. They were using clones.

"Blink! I'm here. What room?" She called out instead of using her comms.

"Here!" Aria's muffled voice came from behind her, so Nyx spun around and headed back at a jog. A door opened to her left and Nyx raised her weapon, ready to shoot in case it was a trap. "Show yourself."

"Over here, and don't you dare shoot at me, it might break a nail or something." Aria called and stuck her hand out in a casual wave.

Nyx snorted. It was definitely Aria. "I don't shoot my friends."

Aria stuck her head out, grinning. "Get your ass in here and save your sister. Or is she your daughter? Whatever. She doesn't have much time. We scanned her. No implants, but Trip says there's too much damage for her to heal herself."

Nyx handed her blaster to Aria as she passed the other woman, then lowered the volume on her comms and closed the channel so her words wouldn't be broadcast to the others. "Where's Sabre?"

"He finished clearing this level, tagged another medical lab like this one, and went on to the next floor.

Dante's got no life signs on the floors below us, so Meyer figured he could handle the sweep solo."

The air in here reeked of charred flesh and fresh blood, the scent overpowering the ship's air scrubbers. There were bloody streaks on the polished metal floor, leading from a spot inside the doorway to where Cris was crouched beside a scorched and bloodied woman wearing a familiar face – hers.

It had been years since they'd allowed her to interact with the other furies, and she'd forgotten how shocking it was to see another version of herself.

She hurried over and dropped to her knees beside Cris. The fury opened her eyes and managed a grim smile. "Don't I know you from somewhere?"

"Could be."

"You came," The fury's voice was weak and getting weaker with every word. She'd taken a blaster bolt to the chest and another to her shoulder.

Nyx reached out to take the fury's uninjured hand. "I told you I would, and brought some friends along with me. Stay alive and I'll introduce you to them."

"She even brought her boyfriend," Cris said.

"Boyfriend?" The fury looked shocked. "They let you date?"

Cris chuckled, but there was worry layered beneath the sound. "No one *lets* her do anything. Nyx is free to make her own choices, and so will you, once we get you fixed up."

"What do you need me to do to make that happen?" she asked.

The team's medic gave her a thin-lipped smile. "Bleed for me."

She looked down at the combat armor that covered most of her body, and tipped her head away from him, offering him her carotid artery. "Do it."

Her comms continued to quietly broadcast constant updates from Eric and the others, but she only paid enough attention to know that Eric had made it to the shuttle bay and was attempting to stop the shuttle from leaving. Dante was helping, using the *Malora's* plasma cannons to fire warning shots and discourage Absalom from trying to escape.

Cris had the equipment already prepared, and all she had to do was hold still while he worked. It was harder to do than she expected—the scent of blood and pain and the sight of the medical implements laid out around her triggered memories she'd done her best to bury since her rescue. She squeezed the fury's hand and focused on her instead of what was happening around them.

"Do you have a name?" she asked the other woman in an attempt to distract them both.

"They called me Echo, just like the others." The fury paused as a fit of coughing seized her, and when she stopped there were fresh flecks of blood on her lips. "It's not a name I want to keep."

"I chose Nyx for myself. You can choose, too."

"I'd like that." The fury winced as Cris pressed a compression injector to her throat and injected her with the first batch of medi-bots.

"She could use a second dose."

"Take whatever you need. I'll heal." She squeezed her clone's hand. "And so will she."

Tranquility filled her and she felt a lightness that had nothing to do with gravity. She'd made the right choice today, she could feel it.

"What does your name mean?"

"Nyx is an ancient goddess from human mythology. She was the goddess of night, and the daughter of chaos." One of the kinder techs had arranged for her to have an old data tablet a long time ago. It had been loaded with random books and information, including poets and a book of mythology. She'd committed them all to memory, but the collection of myths had been one of her favorites.

"Daughter of chaos, huh? Good choice." She coughed again, but this time, it ended quickly, and she didn't cough up more blood.

Cris extracted another vial of her blood and transferred it to the fury. Once that was done, he ran a scanner over the clone, then nodded, his shoulders relaxing a fraction. "She's stabilizing."

"It worked?" Nyx looked down at her clone and had to blink away the tears that blurred her vision.

"It worked. You got here in time." Cris placed a blood-stained hand on her shoulder. "You saved her."

"I couldn't have done it without your help." That truth resonated deep in her heart. She'd been on her own most of her life. There'd never been anyone she could trust – until now. Now she had friends. She had

Eric. And she'd nearly walked away from it all because she hadn't seen it until it was almost too late.

Eric. Her moment of calm evaporated as she grabbed her comms and opened a channel. "Magi, this is Nyx. Things are good here. What's happening?"

"Glad to hear it," Eric responded, his words almost drowned out by the sound of blaster fire. "You want the good news or the bad?"

"Good." She looked at Aria, who was pacing by the door, her fingers drumming on the hilt of her blaster.

"Good news is, I'm not dead."

"And the bad?" Cris asked, projecting his voice to be heard over her comms.

"Neither is Absalom or the two assholes protecting him, and they've got a fully armed shuttle to hide in."

Nyx looked at her companions. "Can you get her back to the *Malora* without my help?"

"We might not be super-soldiers, but we'll manage," Aria drawled and tossed Nyx her blaster. "You're going to need that."

Her clone nodded weakly. "Go. I want to meet this guy of yours when this is over."

Nyx grinned at the fury. "Just remember, he's mine. You'll have to find your own. Magi, I'm coming to you. Hang on."

"Yay, company. I was feeling lonely up here."

Dax broke in. "He's not alone, Nyx. Trinity and I have control of the automated defenses and are giving him remote support."

"It's fun!" Trin called out.

"I'm on my way." She took off at a dead run, covering the distance even faster than the last time, despite the fact she stopped to relieve several corpses of their weapons along the way. Eric had been there for her when she needed him. Now, it was her turn to be there for him.

CHAPTER SIXTEEN

WHEN HE WAS YOUNGER, he'd always taken pride in being the underdog, taking the fight to the big corporations and bringing them down. Today, facing an armed shuttlecraft in a contained space with minimal backup, he decided that his younger self was an idiot.

He'd managed to take down the shuttle's shields with one of his grenades, so now he was picking his targets with care, trying to cripple the ship while Dax and Trinity covered him with the less precise but high-powered defensive array. They were in a messy kind of standoff, but with the *Malora* parked just outside the bay doors, it was only a matter of time before Absalom surrendered. Either that, or an errant blaster bolt would punch a hole in the hull and things would really start to suck, literally.

On impulse he decided to try a new tactic. "Do you really want to die today?"

"I could ask you the same question. I'm not the one

currently vulnerable to vacuum. One shot through the hull and you're a dead man."

He took another shot and then retreated behind the dubious cover of a cargo carry-all. "You kill me, then my team kills you. So, we're back to my question, do you want to die today?"

"Death holds no fear for me."

"Is there a reason you're having a philosophical chat with the enemy, Magi?" Dax asked.

"I told you, it's lonely in here."

"You are a Pain. In. My. Ass." Dax ground out. "Good news, you won't be lonely long. Nyx is coming through that door in about three seconds. We'll cover her entry."

Dax didn't need to have bothered. Nyx came through the door like an avenging angel, a blaster in one hand and a pulse rifle in the other. She moved with deadly grace and speed, running and dodging her way across the bay faster than the shuttle's weapon system could track. She didn't stop shooting as she ran, every shot slamming into the same spot on the shuttle's hull.

She arrived at his side, tracked by a hail of energy bolts that made the wall behind them glow red.

"Hey, lover. Miss me?" She tossed him the pulse rifle she was carrying and unslung another one from her back.

"Always."

She flashed him a smile brighter than a supernova and tipped her head toward the shuttle. "He's in there?"

"Yes. I dropped two of his lackeys before they could get inside, but I counted three inside, Absalom and two others. Their shields are down, but I can't risk using another plasma grenade. One more and the hull's going to buckle, and after the first one they blasted away any cover close enough for me to throw another one accurately."

Her eyes widened and she stared at him for a second in shock. "You set off a grenade in *here*?"

"You're surprised? I thought we already established I'm insane."

She shook her head. "What am I going to do with you?"

"I'm hoping we kick this guy's ass, have a hot shower together, and then lock ourselves in my quarters and stay naked until we get home."

"Magi, this is an open channel. None of us need to hear that," Dante complained.

"Deal with it," Eric shot back then looked at her. "Suggestions on how we get the sardines out of the can?"

"I have no idea what a sardine is, but yeah, I have a plan. You'll like it. Give me a plasma grenade."

"You're both insane," Dax interjected. "And I'm *fraxxing* ordering you both to refrain from blowing up yourselves, or anything else!"

"Commander Rossi, you seem to have forgotten something," Nyx replied in the sweetest voice Eric had ever heard her use.

"What would that be?" Dax demanded.

She held out her hand to Eric and he placed his last plasma grenade in her palm.

"I'm a free agent, Commander. I don't have to follow your orders."

"Dammit, Nyx! Don't get my ensign killed!"

"I don't plan on it."

"Do I get to know the plan?" Eric asked, though he had a good idea what she had in mind. There weren't many things they could do with a plasma grenade, and they all involved moving fast to avoid getting blown up.

"I throw this and we run like hell. I'm fast enough to get us through the doors before it goes off. You got the shields down, so one more hit should cripple them."

"Works for me. Commander, you think you could open the doors for us once we start running?"

"I'm on it," Trinity stated. "I'll close them, too. It'll be faster if I do it from here. You two just focus on getting out of harm's way."

"Thank you, Trin," Nyx said then reached over and grabbed his belt at the back. "Have I mentioned how sexy it is when you get all rough and grabby with me?"

She rolled her eyes and leaned in to kiss him. "Quiet, or Dante will start complaining again."

"Damn right I will. I've backed the *Malora* off in case the hull gives way. All clear and waiting on you two."

"Ready?" she asked him.

He held up a hand and indulged in one last attempt at diplomacy. They needed Absalom alive if at all possible, and once Nyx tossed that grenade, the doctor's chances of survival would drop. "One second. Hey, Doc. Last chance to surrender!"

Absalom responded immediately, his tone both superior and somewhat bored. "The arrival of Subject One hasn't changed the situation. She was my prisoner for years and despite her constant threats against me, she never managed to do me harm. I see no reason why that would change now. She is a blunt instrument, a tool that has outlived her usefulness."

Eric snarled. No one talked about Nyx that way in his hearing. "If you don't kill him, I will."

She winked at him. "You're sexy when you get all growly like that." Then she stood and yelled "I haven't outlived my usefulness yet! I still need to take you down." Then she hurled the grenade, turned, and ran across the shuttle bay so fast all he could do was try and keep his legs under him. Their momentum carried them through the doors and across the hall to slam into the far wall of the corridor – hard. Nyx hit half a step before he did, putting herself between him and the wall.

He managed to catch most of his weight on his arms, bracing himself so he didn't crush her too much. They were both grinning as an explosion rocked the floor beneath their feet, the doors closing as decompression sirens started to scream.

She had never looked so beautiful. Eyes as bright as molten steel, cheeks flushed and smudged with traces of blood he knew wasn't hers. Her black body armor was molded to her body and showed off her curves in a way no military uniform should have managed to do. "You blew a hole in the ship."

"I did."

"You are the sexiest woman in the galaxy right now." Desire swept through him and he moved in close enough his lips brushed hers as he murmured "I love you, my starshine."

"I love you, too, my lunatic."

He kissed her then, both of them laughing and giddy with adrenaline as they held each other tight. Mouths open, tongues tangled, bodies rubbing together despite the armor they both wore. He needed to feel her, to taste her, to prove to himself she was here, alive, well, and his.

He relished every stolen second, knowing it would be a while before they'd have time alone. She brushed his cheek with bloodied fingers, and he knew their time was up.

"Ready to finish the mission?" he asked.

Her lips curled up in a feral smile. "I've waited my whole life for this moment."

"I know."

She cocked her head. "You're not going to remind me you need to interrogate him?"

He knew she had always planned on killing Absalom. As much as they needed him alive to interrogate, he wasn't going to stop her if that's what she needed to do. He shook his head.

"He won't, but I will," Dax chimed in over their still-open comms.

"What's the situation in the shuttle bay, commander?" Eric asked.

"Messy. Someone threw a plasma grenade and blew a hole in the hull," Dax retorted, his tone as dry as dust. "From what we can see on the monitors, the shuttle is crippled but more or less intact. Trinity has deployed repair droids to the breach site and they should have a temporary patch in place shortly. Once we re-pressurize, the two of you, along with myself and Jessop will go in and make arrests."

Nyx nodded. "Trip, Any update on my clone?"

"Sabre and I are taking her to the *Malora*'s med-bay now. She's going to be fine, Nyx. I'll stay with her," Cris replied.

"Thank you."

Eric saw the relief wash over Nyx at the news. It was subtle, but undeniable. After years of hiding her feelings, she was finally letting them show. He took her hand and squeezed it and she flashed him a grateful smile.

"You two stay where you are and guard the door in case they've got pressure suits in the shuttle. Trinity will watch via monitor and let you know if there's any movement. Blink and I are on our way. Sabre, I need you to check the computer situation and make sure our download is going smoothly."

"We're on it, sir." He moved away from Nyx, but kept hold of her hand as they turned and faced the doors. He had no intention of letting go unless they were attacked, and even then, he was ready to shoot one-handed.

HER ENTIRE WORLD had shifted on its axis and she was still trying to find her equilibrium again. Her feelings for Eric, the rescue of her clone, the realization that she wasn't alone anymore, it was a lot to process, and that was before she considered that beyond that door was the man responsible for more suffering and death than he could ever atone for. Not that the bastard would ever feel a moment's guilt for anything he'd done to her, or anyone else.

She was still trying to get her thoughts in order when Dax and Aria arrived. Dax's body armor was scorched across one shoulder, evidence that taking the bridge hadn't gone as easily as they'd hoped.

"You okay, sir?" Eric asked as they fell in behind the two senior teammates.

Dax grunted. "The armor did its job, but I think next time I'll put Strak on the boarding team and babysit the ship myself. I'm getting too old for this crap."

"With respect, sir, I'm older than you and I managed to avoid getting shot," Cris chimed in via comms.

"You had Blink covering your ass, though," Dax replied.

"Are you implying I failed to provide you proper cover, Commander Rossi?" Trin asked over the open channel, her voice dangerously pleasant.

"*Veth*," Dax muttered. "Of course not, Lieutenant West-Rossi. I just didn't duck fast enough."

"Mmhmm." Nyx wasn't sure how, but Trin made the humming noise sound like a threat.

Dax gestured them forward and they moved as a group toward the door in silence. It fascinated her how the team could switch from friendly banter to deadly intent so quickly.

"Patching completed, pressurization in progress. There's no movement from the shuttle, and they are not answering my hails."

"Weapons?" Dax asked.

"Inoperable. We have them and they know it," Trinity stated.

"Which means Absalom will be livid and trying to think of a way to make us pay for this. Be extremely cautious," Nyx said.

"Noted," Aria said.

"It will be safe to enter in twenty seconds," Trinity said.

"Open the doors in ten. We need to be in position before they have a chance to move," Dax said.

Everyone stood in their positions, ready to move or shoot the second the doors opened. Eric stood beside her, his silent presence a gratifying comfort. She shifted closer and bumped her shoulder to his, then moved away again and he grinned without looking at her.

The doors opened as Trin's countdown ended, and they moved through to take up new positions inside, the four of them fanning out to cover the shuttle door.

"I am Commander Dax Rossi of Nova Force, and you are under arrest, Dr. Absalom. I suggest you surrender, now. You're out of options."

"I am never without options, Commander. However, at this time, I will elect to surrender myself into your custody, if only to put an end to the wanton destruction of my property." Absalom spoke so casually he might have been discussing lunch plans instead of his imminent arrest.

Nyx tightened her grip on her weapon and waited. She'd expected to feel anxious, or angry, but all she felt was a fierce sense of satisfaction. At that moment, she knew she wouldn't kill him. She didn't have to. He'd suffer more if she left him alive and destined to spend the rest of his life rotting away in a cell somewhere.

The door to the shuttle opened and he stepped into view with a confident air that didn't match his current circumstances. He was of average height, a bit on the thin side, with angular features and a high forehead. His dark hair was starting to thin at the temples, and his mouth was pressed into a thin, unhappy line.

He looked diminished somehow, as if the act of surrendering had stripped him of some of his power and authority. Or maybe he hadn't changed at all. It was because she was seeing him from a new perspective. She wasn't his prisoner anymore. He was hers.

They held their places, weapons held at the ready as Absalom descended to the shuttle bay floor.

"Where are the rest of your crew, doctor?" Dax asked.

The doctor's mouth twisted up into a brief and unpleasant smile. "Dead men tell no tales."

"Son of a starbeast, he killed them," Aria muttered so softly Nyx could barely hear it even with her enhanced senses.

"Blink, secure our prisoner and scan him. Magi, you and Nyx check the shuttle."

"Yessir," Eric jogged over to the crippled ship and she kept pace beside him, not even looking at the doctor as they moved past.

She touched Eric's arm as they approached. "Let me go first. My senses are better than yours and I don't trust him."

"Booby traps?" Eric asked.

"Could be."

He made a sweeping bow. "Then by all means, ladies first."

The inside of the shuttle was in good shape considering the external damage it had suffered. There were two bodies sprawled on the floor near the cockpit, as if they'd been shot by someone seated at the controls.

"He killed them once he realized it wasn't going to go his way. Just turned around and opened fire." Eric had entered behind her and come to the same conclusion.

She made her way over to the bodies, noting they were the same height and weight. She'd guess they were clones, but there was no way to be certain.

Absalom had shot them both in the head at close range, and the damage was extensive. "I think these two were clones, like the ones I saw on the lower levels."

"Makes sense. This was his personal ship. He'd only want people he trusted or could completely control this close to him." Eric grimaced. "Atmo-scrubbers must be offline. It reeks in here."

The scents of scorched meat and death were a cloying miasma that she had to work to shut out so she could focus on the rest of their surroundings. Gingerly she stepped over the bodies while shifting her vision to include the infrared spectrum. Instantly she spotted several thin beams crisscrossing the cockpit door.

"Don't move." She warned Eric.

"*Fraxx*. What is it?"

"Not sure yet, but be ready to run."

Eric tapped out something on his comms and hers buzzed several times in quick succession. "Now the others know there's a potential problem and will clear the area."

"Good." She took a few slow breaths and then leaned into the cockpit, careful not to step inside or break any of the beams. A quick scan told her everything she needed to know. Micro-explosives were scattered across the console and seats like confetti.

"Out. Now. Go!"

She turned to find Eric already sprinting for the exit. She caught up to him outside the shuttle and grabbed his hand as they ran, both of them laughing as they sprinted across the shuttle bay for the second time that day. They didn't stop running until they cleared the doors and once again bounced off the wall on the far side of the corridor outside the shuttle bay.

Eric groaned and shook his head as he stepped away from the wall. "This is getting to be a habit."

"What happened in there?" Dax asked.

"Micro-explosives," she explained.

Everyone turned to stare at Absalom, who was standing nearby already in hand and ankle restraints. The doctor merely shrugged a little. "We are enemies, are we not?"

She tensed and Eric placed a hand on her back, a steadying gesture that helped her keep her temper – barely.

"Strak, it's time to call this in. Let HQ know what we found, and who we have in custody. They can send people to tear this ship apart. I want every corpse identified, every file logged, and every square centimeter of this ship examined, then dismantled." Dax looked squarely at Absalom and deadpanned, "After all, we are enemies."

Nyx squared her shoulders and stepped into the doctor's line of sight. "I told you I'd bring you down someday. Operation Fury is over. I'm free, and so is the last fury."

"You are a simple tool, and a poor one at that. You think you've stopped me, but there is no stopping what has been set in motion, it is too vast a plan for you to comprehend it, Subject One."

Eric slammed his fist into Absalom's smug face hard

enough he staggered back a few steps. "Her name is Nyx."

"And I am not anyone's tool. Not anymore." She turned to smile at Eric. "Thank you, lover."

He winked. "You're welcome."

"Everyone back to the *Malora*. We're headed home." Dax pointed to the doctor. "You walk beside me. I see you so much as twitch, and a punch to the face will be the least of your problems." He lifted his blaster then lowered it again. "Clear?"

"As polished crystal." Absalom managed to flick his fingers in a 'carry-on' gesture that set her teeth on edge.

She'd made her choice, but part of her still wanted to hurt him for all he'd done to her and the others, including the men and women with her. If anyone but her had gone into that shuttle, things could have turned out very differently.

Without a word she reached out and stroked her fingers over the back of Eric's hand and smiled. Somehow, it looked like the two of them were going to have their chance at 'later' after all.

CHAPTER SEVENTEEN

While Dante plotted a course for home and Dax and Trinity secured their prisoner in the brig, Eric went to his workspace to check on the data transfer he'd initiated when they'd initially boarded the *Enigma.* He'd partitioned off a section of the ship's computer as a kind of digital quarantine, ensuring that nothing his sprites had collected would be able to infect other parts of the system.

It didn't look like they'd lost much to the system wipe that had been triggered by their arrival. He'd been expecting that and reprogrammed some of his sprites to shut down any attempt to destroy the data.

"Did you get what you needed?" Nyx asked. She'd followed him in and was standing in the middle of the cluttered space, arms folded as if she didn't want to touch anything.

"I think so. It's too much to sort through, but that's good news. Last time all I managed to retrieve were fragments. This should give us solid intel on what Absalom was up to, and how he fits in with the Gray Men. He has to be working with them and his older self, but how? And where are they hiding?"

"Hopefully, the answers are in there, somewhere. Along with enough information to make everyone back at HQ happy." Nyx stepped in close and laid her head on his shoulder, her arms looping around his waist. "We haven't talked about it, but I know what you risked to come after me."

"And I'd do it again if I had to."

She chuckled. "Lunatic."

"Ah, but I'm *your* lunatic." And he planned on keeping it that way. He pulled out his comms and opened a channel to Dax. "Sir. The data collection looks good. We didn't lose much, and the quarantine I set up is holding. When do you want us to report for debrief?"

"Debrief is in two hours. Trip has the fury stabilized. She's currently sleeping. He'll inform us when she's awake and ready to talk to us."

"Thank you, sir. Nyx and I will see you in two hours." He turned off his comm and turned his head to nuzzle her cheek. "We've got a little time. Which do you want first, food or a hot shower?"

She sighed. "There really needs to be a way to do both at the same time."

"That is a brilliant idea. Come with me." It was time to show her another of the *Malora's* luxuries – the sim pods.

He hustled her out in the corridor and broke into a

jog, heading for the galley.

"Where are we going and why are you in such a hurry all of a sudden?" she asked.

"The last time we were on the *Malora*, an IAF cruiser appeared and stole you away from me. This time, I'm not taking any chances. We're hitting the galley for supplies, and then we're going to find a place with plenty of hot water and a locking door."

"Oh! Well, why didn't you say so?" She ran past him, laughing. "I want cupcakes!"

He loved hearing her laugh. It was a sound he hoped he'd hear more often now. He knew she'd need time to heal and come to terms with everything, but now she would have that time. *They* had time.

They loaded up a couple of trays with whatever they could find or have the food dispensers make quickly. Mugs of cocoa, cupcakes and leftovers from the cooler, snacks from the pantry, and a pint of chocolate ice cream he'd stashed in the back of the freezer.

Aria came in as they were finishing. "Holy *fraxx*, did you leave anything for the rest of us?"

Nyx held out her tray to Aria. "You saved my clone. You can have anything you like."

Aria froze. "I didn't save her. That was Trip. I'm the one who shot her."

"I know." Nyx set down the tray and moved to stand in front of Aria, looking uncertain. "May I hug you?"

"Uh. Sure."

Eric's heart almost broke as he watched the woman

he loved try to reach out to someone else for the first time.

The two hugged for an awkward moment, but when they let go, they were both smiling. "You did what you had to do to protect yourself and your teammate. I don't blame you for that. You didn't shoot to kill. You tried to protect her, too. I saw the bodies. You and your team went for headshots."

Aria's smile flickered. "I screwed up. I thought she'd have body armor like the rest of them."

"Absalom wouldn't waste resources on someone he considered expendable."

Aria grimaced. "No one is expendable, except maybe the doctor and that brunette bitch who sicced your clone on us. I swear she laughed when she did it."

"Can you describe her for me?"

Blink tapped a finger to her temple. "Don't need to. She was one of the people you identified for us. I compared the image you shared with the one I recorded today and confirmed it. Vivian Davros."

"Absalom's personal assistant. At least, I think that's what she was. She wasn't part of the experiments, but she was always nearby, updating him and implementing his orders."

"And she got away in the other shuttle." Aria grimaced. "I'm going to add her name to my personal grudge list. But first, I need to eat."

Nyx picked up her tray again. "I left two cupcakes in the cooler. They're hidden behind the produce."

"Perfect! Thank you."

They left Aria to her cupcakes and made their way to the elevator. The sim-pods were one of the true luxuries to be found on the *Malora,* allowing the crew to spend their off-duty time relaxing or even training in a variety of sims.

"This one will work, It's the largest one. Dante uses it for hand-to-hand training sometimes."

He handed his tray to Nyx, then stole a quick kiss. Her lips were sweet and slightly sticky, and she tasted of chocolate.

"You ate one already?"

"It was delicious. If you don't hurry, I'm going to eat another one while we stand here."

The idea of her licking the frosting off a cupcake without using her hands had him scrambling to get the program started.

He scrolled through several options and found one that sounded perfect. "Computer, run program – Private bathing suite – romantic subroutine."

"Romantic sub-routine? On a military vessel?" Nyx asked.

"Over the years we've added our own programs. I don't know who added that one, and honestly, I don't want to think about it too much. Let's just enjoy it."

"You'll kill for them, die for them, but you don't want to think about them having sex?"

"Exactly."

"Your program is running. You may now enter, Ensign Erben," the computer informed them as the door slid open to reveal a palatial bathing chamber.

"Now this is perfect." He took one of the trays from Nyx and stepped inside. Fragrant steam drifted in the air, carrying a subtle blend of soft spices and warm wax as it dripped from the dozens of white candles that lit the room. The floor and walls were white marble shot through with ribbons of dark green. And thick towels in the same colors were stacked on benches that lined the walls. Most of the room was taken up by a pool of slowly swirling water. It was the source of the steam that filled the room.

"Computer, add a low table to one side of the pool suitable for serving food and beverages while the occupants bathe."

A marble table appeared exactly as specified, and he set first his tray, then Nyx's. By the time he straightened, she was unlacing her boots.

"None of this is real?" She asked.

"It's real enough, but only when the projectors are on. It's all holographic. Don't ask me to explain it, because I have no idea how it works. The only things real in here are you, me, and the items we brought in with us."

"Which explains the food." She kicked off her boots, then growled in frustration as she tried to free herself from the body-hugging armor.

"There's a knack to it." He moved to her side and showed her the order to undo the fastenings. She watched, and instead of taking over, she started undoing his armor the same way.

He undressed her quickly, shrugging out of his own

gear without a care for where it fell. He had planned for them to eat first, but that plan went up in flames the second he caught a glimpse of bare shoulders and soft skin. It felt like an eternity since he'd held her last, and he'd feared he'd never get to hold her again.

He was hard and aching by the time she got his pants off, and the vision she made as she knelt at his feet, helping him step out of his clothes, was enough to make his cock throb.

She flashed him a wicked little smile as she leaned in and feathered several kisses to the crown of his shaft.

"You keep doing that and we might never get to use that pool," he warned her.

"Why can't we do both?" She rose to her feet with a predator's grace and took him by the hand. She led him to the stairs leading into the pool and then down into the water, every step she took hiding more of her beautiful body beneath the water.

When he reached the third step, she placed a hand on his chest and pushed lightly. "Sit. I have a plan."

"Am I going to like this plan?"

She nodded. "Sit."

Veth, he loved it when she got like this, and she knew it, too. He sat on the top stair, the hot water lapping at his thighs. She moved between his legs and settled on one of the lower stairs and leaned down to take his cock into her mouth, her fingers firmly gripping his shaft.

"*Fraxx*, that's good." He laid a hand gently on the back of her head and closed his eyes, letting the heat of her mouth and the touch of her hands banish any other thoughts.

She swiped her tongue down the underside of his cock to where her fingers held him, then worked her way back up with feathery kisses that were too light to do anything but tease. By the time she reached his crown again he was arching off the stairs. She laughed as she took him deep into her mouth, the vibration of it nearly making him cum on the spot.

He groaned her name and she drew him in deeper, all the way to the back of her throat, her cheeks hollowing with the suction as she took him to the edge of his control.

"No more of that or you're going to break me."

She lifted her head and laughed. "I thought that was the point?"

"But not yet. First, I get to break you." He tugged her into his arms and kissed her, her warm, wet curves pressing against him, tempting him to tug her onto his lap and take her right there on the stairs. *Next time.*

Now he knew there would be a next time. If the universe was kind, they'd have years of next times. He liked that idea.

SHE LOVED the way he kissed her with all his focus, like she was the only star in his orbit. She rubbed her wet body against his, feeling the warmth and strength of him as he claimed his mouth with a singled minded fervor that set her blood ablaze.

She knew he planned to make her come before he fucked her, but she didn't want to wait. She twined her arms around his neck and drew him down the stairs, until he was seated low enough in the water she could sit in his lap without leaving the comfort of the pool.

"This is not what I had in mind," he stated, amusement and desire deepening his voice to a sexy rumble that turned her mind to mush.

"Play later. Love me now." She kissed him again. "Please?"

He cupped her face in his hands and gazed into her eyes, his own burning with something far deeper than need. "You never have to ask me to love you, starshine."

She shivered slightly as the weight of his words settled around her, wrapping her in warmth and light. "I love you, too. I didn't know I could feel like this."

He reached between them to press a hand to her chest, over her heart. "You're not a machine, Nyx. Nor a tool, or a possession. You're a woman." He kissed her softly. "My woman."

"And you're my lunatic."

"Always," he whispered.

He kissed his way from her lips to her throat and she leaned back to let him roam farther, until his mouth was on her breasts, nibbling and sucking on them until she was quivering with need. She knelt facing him, her legs spanning his thighs, her pussy brushing against his cock with every move they made.

He slid a hand between them, his clever fingers seeking out her clit, making her shudder and grind herself against his hand. The warm water was like a gentle caress across her skin, heightening every decadent sensation until she was drunk with desire. He would have continued pleasuring her until she came, but she didn't want to wait. She needed him, all of him, now.

Without a word, she rose up on her knees, arching her hips until the thick head of his cock bumped against her entrance. "Need you."

His breath quickened and he kissed her, his hands landing on her hips as he drew her down onto his cock. He entered her slowly, not stopping until he was buried balls deep inside her.

She moaned into his mouth and rocked her hips, teasing them both.

"Not slow. Not this time," He tightened his hold and raised her a few inches, then arched himself up and into her in a hard thrust that made her gasp.

"Yes!"

That was all the encouragement he needed. He powered into her again and again, the water overflowing the edges of the pool as they made love. Her inner walls flexed around his cock, milking him with every stroke.

It was different this time, more intense. Their feelings for each other stoking the fires of their passion until it was like standing in the heart of a star. "Love you," she moaned the words as she rode him, every thrust bringing her closer to orgasm.

Her nails raked his back as she clung to him in a frantic dance of give-and-take that ended when she came apart in a breath-stealing release that left her dazed and panting. Eric didn't last more than a few more strokes before he came, too, his entire body rising, lifting them both partially out of the water as he shuddered and collapsed back into the pool with a satisfied groan.

"We really need a copy of this program," he muttered as he cuddled her close.

"I agree, but I don't think it was the program that made it so amazing."

She let herself drift for a long, leisurely moment, her thoughts and body floating in a pleasant fugue that lasted until Eric asked the question she'd known would come eventually.

"What happened today? When you started to say you loved me, you had this look like you knew it was the last thing you'd ever get to say."

"I thought it was. I was programmed with a shutdown command. Two, actually. At least, that's what Absalom always claimed. One to deactivate me temporarily. The other would kill me. He used the commands to control me and all the furies. He didn't need to implant us with those explosive devices you told me about. He could shut us down with a word."

He tensed, his arms tightening around her to the

point she couldn't move. "Why the hell would you go after him alone if you knew you could be stopped by anyone with the code?"

"They were a carefully guarded secret. Absalom was the only one who knew mine. I know that, because the guards would bitch about how much easier it would be to control me if they could have the codes."

"It was still an insane risk."

She shrugged. "I had to try. I knew I'd likely only get one shot at him before he used the override, but I never thought about him using the intercom. If the command had worked like it should have…" In hindsight she knew it was a stupid mistake, one that had nearly cost her everything.

"You should have told me."

"What? Tell you I had a secret override code implanted in my programming and anyone who figured out what it was could literally turn me off and reset me, or even kill me?" She shook her head. "It was too big a risk to let anyone know. What I still don't understand is why it didn't work."

"I don't know. Maybe they deactivated yours while you were being tested and assessed back on Astek station. Son of a—the Reapers. Yeah. I bet that's what happened."

Her thoughts slammed into a jumbled wreck like a mag-train that jumped the tracks. "What? It's fixable? And what about reapers?"

"The Reaper Project was another assassin for hire setup the Grays were running. Two cyborgs programmed and controlled to obey their handlers. They're free now, but I read a little about them when I was trying to track down the Fury Project."

"And these Reapers had their codes deactivated?"

Eric nodded. "With the help of a doctor on Astek, actually. Caldwell's sister. She works with a former cybernetics tech and become something of a cyborg health expert. *Veth*. I'd forgotten all about it until now. I'm sorry. If I'd remembered sooner…"

"If I had trusted you enough to tell you, you'd have remembered." She sighed and shifted her weight, settling deeper into his arms.

"Doesn't Trip's sister run the med-center Dr. Li works at?" It pained her to think that Tyra would have altered something in her coding and not even mentioned it to her. It didn't feel like something the other woman would do, but the pieces all fit. When she got back to Astek, she'd have to find out.

"She does, and I know what you're thinking, but I can't see Tyra doing something like that. We'll figure it out once we're home."

"Home." She sounded the word out carefully. "I like the sound of that." It was the first time the word had meant something to her. Astek was her home, or it could be.

"About that. I was thinking, since you're probably not going to be Nova Force's guest for much longer, you'll need a place to stay."

"I'll need a job, too, or eating and rent are going to be a problem."

"Astek gave all of their cyborgs backpay when they were freed. Since you were never freed, I think we should see about collecting what you're owed. That should take care of your financial security. You could stay anywhere you wanted." He cleared his throat. "Even go travel the galaxy for a bit if that's what you wanted."

"Alone?" The idea of traveling was intriguing, but she didn't want to do it on her own. She wanted to do it with Eric.

"Alone? No. Not if I have anything to say about it. But this is all new for you, so I don't want you feeling like you have to stay with me." He stroked her cheek, softly. "But I want that. I want you with me, starshine."

"Me, too." She took a deep breath and turned to nuzzle his hand, hiding her face. "I don't know what my life is going to look like yet, but I do know I want you in it."

"If you move in with me, we could be part of each other's lives."

Her heart beat so hard against her ribs she thought it might burst with joy. "I want that. I want to go home with you."

"And I want to *make* a home with you."

She looked into his face and saw her future in his smile. She knew who she was, and what she wanted. There were no more doubts. She was finally free to follow her heart, and she knew exactly where it would lead her – home, with the man she loved.

CHAPTER EIGHTEEN

THE BRIEFING ROOM of the Malora had been transformed for the night. The drab walls had been festooned with silver and gold streamers, and there was a holographic banner projected across one wall that read "Good Luck!"

Eric leaned against a wall and watched as Nyx mingled and laughed with his friends and teammates. She'd transformed since returning to Astek, her spirit lighter and her smile coming easier with every day that passed. It wouldn't always be this easy. She still had demons to fight, but she was strong and determined to make a life for herself, and he was just as determined to help her achieve that goal.

Tonight, they were here to say goodbye to Shadow. The last surviving fury was bound for Haven, a cyborg colony that had been created for cyborgs like her, victims of the Gray Men who were used and abused long after all the cyborgs were supposed to have been freed. The invitation had been for both Nyx and Shadow, but only Shadow had accepted. Nyx had made her choice the day they'd captured Absalom, and Eric would make sure she never regretted her choice.

Dante's son, Nico, wandered by with a plate stacked high with food. "Good food!"

"Did you leave any for the rest of us?" Eric teased.

The kid grinned. "Only if you get there before Dante."

"We still on for a robotic repair session tomorrow? If you're going to keep crashing that bot, you need to learn how to repair it yourself."

"I'll be there!"

The kid was gone a second later, no doubt to tell his parents about both the food and the training session. Tyra hugged him and directed a smile in Eric's direction. The kid had been a street rat when Tyra found him, and he was still trying to find a way to leave that part of his life behind him. Eric understood better than most the temptation to fall into old habits, and he did what he could to keep Nico busy and away from trouble.

"What was that about?" Nyx asked, sliding in next to him and resting her head on his shoulder, though she was careful not to put too much pressure on the area where his new tattoo sat. It was a stylized image of a winged woman emerging from a storm cloud to ascend into a clear sky. Nyx had one just like it.

"Robotics repair session tomorrow. Dante wants

Nico to learn about consequences. He broke his racing bot again, so I'm going to show him how to fix it."

"It's a good lesson. Good skillset, too. He's a lucky kid to have people who care so much about him."

"They care about you, too. Tyra already came by to ask how you're doing."

Nyx smiled. "You mean she wants to know if I'm ready to meet her friends at the Nova Club. I know it's been hard on her, not telling them about me. Echo was their friend, and seeing me is going to bring up a lot of complicated feelings, but it can't be easy for her to keep my presence here a secret, either."

"That's part of it. She's still feeling guilty she didn't know they deactivated your codes without telling you, too."

Nyx shrugged dismissively. "It wasn't her fault. Not everyone is as caring or careful, as she is." She glanced over at Tyra. "I'll talk to her. I don't want her feeling bad about something she had no control over. As for the other issue." She looked up at him and smiled a little. "I guess it's time I met the cyborgs from the Nova Club. I can't stay hidden from them forever. We're all just going to have to work through the weirdness."

"You sure?" He didn't want her taking on too much, too soon. As strong as she was, he knew none of this was easy for her. Plus, he'd come across some worrying intel about the Nova club. Someone was spying on them. He'd sent his friends what he had, along with a warning, but he didn't want Nyx getting caught in the middle of another crisis so soon.

"I'm sure. But not until after Shadow leaves." There was a hint of sadness in her voice, but there was acceptance, too.

"She's going to a good place. The Vardarians are decent beings, and the cyborgs there have formed a solid community."

"I know." She shot him an amused glance. "You keep telling me. And your friend Phaedra is there. I'm not worried about Shadow. She's going to be fine. And we've got an invitation to visit once she's settled in."

"We do. I'm looking forward to it. I haven't taken leave in more than a year. It would be nice to breathe real atmosphere for a while."

She looked dubious. "Air is air, isn't it?"

"You'll see. Being on a planet is very different from being on a ship or a station like this one."

Dax rapped his knuckles on the wall and everyone settled into an expectant silence. "Shadow, we all just wanted to wish you a safe journey, and a peaceful start to your new life on Liberty."

There was a collective surge of well wishes and agreement, and Shadow ducked her head to hide a blush.

"We're also here for another reason. Nyx, will you come over here, please?"

Nyx straightened and shot him a confused look.

"Surprise," he winked at her. "Go on."

"Nyx. You've been a guest of Nova Force since you're arrival on the station. We thought it was time that changed." Dax held up an ID badge and a keycard.

"These are for you. You're now officially registered as Erben's partner, which makes you the bravest woman on the station."

There was another round of cheering, this one louder and full of laughter.

"Thank you." Nyx took the offered items and beamed at everyone around her. "But you've got it backward. Eric is the brave one."

More laughter, and then Dax pulled out a data tablet and presented it to her.

"What's this?" she asked.

"A job offer. You don't have to give me an answer now, but you've been invited to join Nova Force, as a consultant. You're the closest thing we have to an expert on the Gray Men." Dax looked around the room, his expression somber. "The fight is only going to get harder from now on. I've spoken to Colonel Bahl. Things are going to change. The gloves are coming off, team. New rules. New goals." He glanced at Nyx. "New allies."

"I'd go on missions? Work with your team?"

"That's the plan," Dax said, and Eric nodded to her.

"We already picked out a nickname for you," Dante announced.

"C'mon, Chaos. Say yes. This team needs more estrogen!" Aria added.

Nyx looked back at Eric, her gray eyes shining. "I could make a difference."

The moment she said those words, he knew what

her answer would be. Only she didn't get a chance to accept before everyone's comms went off at once.

It was a summons for a briefing. High priority.

"Well, at least we're in the right place," Dante muttered. He turned to Tyra and kissed her. "I got to go to work, Shortcake. See you at home, later?"

"Later. Come on, Nico. Party's over. Yes, you can take your plate with you."

Dax was still reading and spoke without looking up from his comm. "Nyx and Shadow, you're going to want to stay for this. Blink, secure the room. Magi, the Colonel is going to need a holo-link, make it happen."

In a matter of seconds, the table was cleared off, the chairs rearranged, and everyone took their seats. Nyx stood behind him, her hand on his shoulder, and Shadow leaned up against the wall behind Cris.

Colonel Bahl's hologram shimmered into existence at the far end of the table. She looked around the room, wincing slightly when she spotted the decorations still in place. "Sorry to interrupt, but I wanted you all to hear the news from me, first."

"What the *fraxx* happened, Colonel?" Dax asked, his voice edged in ice. He clearly knew more than the rest of them already.

"Five hours ago, Dr. Jules Absalom collapsed in his cell. Medics were dispatched immediately, but he has remained non-responsive despite all attempts at treatment."

"Is he dying?" Dax asked.

"In some ways, he's already dead. There's almost no higher brain function at all."

"How?" Dax asked.

Bahl frowned. "We don't know that, either. Halverson is too busy declaring his innocence to be of much use. They were only a few hours away from IAF HQ when this happened, we're doing interviews and trying to determine what happened, but it's going to take time."

"He should never have been allowed to take Absalom in the first place." Dax said. "If the General hadn't been trying to take the credit for the doctor's capture and showboating by delivering the prisoner himself—" It was rare for Dax to lose his temper in front of a senior officer this way, but Bahl just nodded in understanding.

"I agree. But two colonels and a commander still hold less power than one general, even one as politically motivated as Halverson."

"Sorry, ma'am." Dax apologized.

"I'm pissed off, too, Commander. And I will make sure that man is never allowed to interfere in another Nova Force matter."

Bahl steepled her fingers in front of her, and the lines in her face deepened. "There's more you need to know. During the medical scans of the prisoner, we found something unusual."

Cris stiffened. "What did you find? He was scanned several times, both before and after coming on board the *Malora*."

"This item was designed not to be detected by normal scanners. From what we can determine, it's an implant created from Absalom's own cells."

Eric leaned forward. "Does it have a data port?"

"It does." Bahl confirmed. "You know what it is?"

"I know what it might be, but it's a rumor, a myth. No one's ever seen it done."

"What is it?" Dax asked.

"Next-generation cyber-jockey stuff. Tech built on a cellular lattice of the donor's own tissue to create undetectable implants."

Bahl nodded. "That would match with what we know so far. But what would be the purpose? We know this version of Absalom is a clone. We've already done a genetic match to verify that."

"The idea was to create implants that couldn't be detected. A cyber-jockey could pass as a norm—uh, a regular being. There are plenty of places that restrict access to people with implants for security reasons." He hadn't even been allowed to set foot on Bellex 3 during a recent mission because the corporate heads were worried about corporate espionage.

"So until we remove it, we won't know what it's real purpose is." Bahl said.

"If you remove it, it will have to be done carefully. You said all his higher functions are gone?"

"More or less, yes."

Eric's stomach twisted. "So, all that's left is a shell. The consciousness is gone."

Everyone turned to stare at him. "Gone where, exactly?" Dax asked.

"Somewhere else. The datasphere maybe. Or a new receptacle. It's theoretically possible, but everyone who tried has died. Plus, there are rules against it. A lot of rules."

"You're talking about digitizing consciousness?" Bahl asked.

"He already did it once, sort of, with V.I.D.A. She's a fully sentient AI, and he created her years ago. If he's been working on it all this time..." Eric nodded. "Yeah, it's possible. The Grays don't care about rules, and they've got the money and means to make it happen."

"Son of a bitch," Dante growled from the far end of the table.

"That is an alarming theory." Bahl stated. "And for now, that's all it is, a theory. But it's a good one. Thank you, Ensign."

Eric nodded. "If I'm right, he'll have needed access to a datasphere to make his escape. He didn't have that on the *Malora*, or while he was held here on Astek. We made sure of that. But if the ship he was on was close enough for him to access the local datasphere, it's possible that's what happened."

"I'll have someone check and see exactly what restrictions were in place around his cell. He should have been on full lockdown, but clearly, mistakes were made."

"That's all we have for now. I wanted you all to get a full briefing, and I'll continue to update you personally.

Nyx and Shadow, we'll do all we can to protect you both, though once Shadow is on Liberty, you'll be out of our jurisdiction. I will notify the colony leaders about the situation before your arrival.

"Thank you," Shadow inclined her head.

"We're entering a new stage now. The stakes are higher, and it's clear our adversaries are willing to go to any lengths to protect themselves. From now on there will be no more fact-finding missions or interference from anyone outside of Nova Force. Oversight will be streamlined, and the chain of command will be direct from me to Commander Rossi and down from there. Colonel Archer will be part of the command structure, but only so that he can provide support as needed for your missions. From now on, this team has one target, the Gray Men. All other investigations will be handled by other teams."

"Yes, ma'am."

"I believe you are the best qualified, most capable team in Nova Force's history. If anyone can beat these sons of starbeasts, it's you. I'll be in touch soon."

There was a chorus of "Yes ma'am" and "thank you, ma'am" as the colonel's hologram faded from view.

Eric turned to look at Nyx. She hadn't moved or spoken during the briefing, except to squeeze his shoulder when she realized Absalom might be alive and free. "You okay?"

"No. That bastard is still out there. He got away because I didn't kill him when I had the chance."

"He got away because Halverson is a *fraxxing* idiot,"

he corrected her. "You did the right thing. Never doubt it."

She didn't look convinced. "When we find him the next time, do we just take him into custody again? Is that how this is going to go?"

Dax got to his feet. "No. We're not going to win if we keep playing by the old rules. When we find a threat, we remove it. Permanently."

Nyx straightened and pivoted to face Dax. "In that case, I accept your job offer, sir. I mean, unless Eric doesn't think it's a good idea."

Eric rose and pulled her in close. "I think it's a great idea. This way, I can keep you out of trouble."

She laughed and wrapped her arms around him. "I think you've got that backward. I'm not the lunatic in this relationship, It's my job to keep *you* out of trouble."

"You're hired. But I should warn you, it's a lifetime contract."

She kissed him before answering. "Sign me up."

Aria was sitting next to them and burst out laughing. "Did you just ask…"

He grinned and kissed Nyx hard. "I did. And she said yes."

All around the table were groans mixed with laughter.

"You're a *fraxxing* lunatic. You know that, right?" Dante rumbled.

Nyx frowned. "Did I miss something?"

"Your lunatic just proposed to you," Aria said, trying, and failing, to keep from laughing.

"Oh!" Nyx held up her left hand and wiggled her fingers. "Does that mean I get a ring, like Trinity's?"

He hadn't planned on doing this yet, but he already knew this was what he wanted. Nyx had started out as his mission, but now she was his destiny. He took her hand and kissed it. "We'll pick one out together, starshine."

"Together," she agreed. "Always."

BONUS SCENE - SABRE

THE PARTY WOUND DOWN FAIRLY QUICKLY after the Colonel's news, with everyone scattering to process the information in their own way. Kurt contemplated going back to his quarters but decided to work instead. He needed to start working out a training program for Nyx. Officially she was a civilian consultant, but there wasn't much about the cyborg that was civilian *anything*.

He settled in at his work station on the Malora and started brainstorming on a pad of paper with an old-fashioned stylus. It was a habit he'd had since he was a kid. He'd been taught to read with wooden blocks his father had carved for him and learned to write on reams of homemade paper. It had been a simple, but boring life, and he'd signed on with the IAF two days, four hours and sixteen minutes after he'd reached the minimum age. It had taken him two days to reach a town big enough to even have a recruitment office, and he'd sat outside the door until they'd opened it the next morning.

He stopped writing and leaned back in the chair, suddenly amused. He'd thought he was signing on for a lifetime of travel, tech, and adventure, and here he was, fifteen years later, writing with a stylus and thinking back fondly to his days on the family farm. At least then, trouble was easy to identify. He could recognize every predatory species in the area on sight or even by their tracks. He'd known their habits and haunts, the prey they preferred, even the time of day they hunted.

Since joining Nova Force, he'd learn to hunt a different kind of predator. The sentient kind. They were trickier, crueler, and far more difficult to predict, but he'd gotten good at it. Until now. He tossed down his stylus and grunted in frustration. How the *fraxx* were they going to find the Grays if they'd figured out how to move their consciousness across from body to body? Not that they were sure that's what was happening, but until an hour ago, he couldn't have imagined it would even be possible. Illegal cloning, Sentient AI's, and now this. The Gray Men were getting more dangerous - and more desperate.

They had inside help, too. Probably from more than one source. Eric's discovery that someone was spying on the cyborgs at the Nova Club was disturbing enough, but it was also part of a larger pattern. The Grays were gathering intelligence on anyone they deemed a threat, and that was going to make them even harder to track down.

He picked up the stylus again. That was a problem for another day. Tonight, all he needed was to start making plans for bringing Nyx up to speed. She was a unique asset, and with the right training, she might make the difference in the coming fight against the Gray Men.

He'd filled most of a page of notes when he heard footsteps coming down the corridor. He checked the time – it was after ten, and there was only one other person who'd be working this late. "Fido, what the hell are you doing here? Don't you have a wife to get home to, man?"

Dax appeared in the doorway a few seconds later. "Trin and I just finished cleaning up after the party. I had a feeling I'd find you here, though." He paused. "Got a minute?"

"Come on in. If I had known you were going to clean up tonight, I'd have stayed to help out."

"It didn't take long. Dante took most of the food with him, and Nyx claimed whatever was left. Between the two of them, we might have to get a second food dispenser for the *Malora*."

Kurt tapped the paper in front of him. "I was making notes on a training program for her. I should start another list with the changes we're going to need to make to the ship now that we've got another couple on board. Reconfigure Erben's quarters, add another food dispenser and maybe increase the amount of food we store on board."

Dax took a seat across from him. "Been a lot of changes lately. Do you think the team's handling it all well?"

He looked his commander and friend in the eye, reading the micro-expressions and the shadows in Dax's eyes. "I think they're handling it fine. I also think you didn't come here to talk to me about team morale."

Dax snorted in wry amusement. "How many times have I told you not to read me like that?"

"As many times as I've told you that it's my job to know what you need and make it happen, and that means listening to what you say and what you haven't said." He reached into the bottom drawer of his desk and pulled out a flask and two metal cups. "And based on what you haven't said out loud, I'm guessing we're going to need a drink."

"Smug is not a good look for you." Dax tapped the cup closest to him. "But you're right. Hit me."

He poured them both two fingers of the fifteen-year-old Scotch and raised his glass. "What shall we drink to?"

"To our friends. The only ones we can *fraxxing* trust right now."

They drank, and Kurt sat back, waiting for Dax to explain. Dax took another drink before he said a word, then sighed. "Sorry, I'm in a mood tonight. It was supposed to be a good night, but we don't seem to get many of those these days."

"We win some, we lose some. Nyx and Shadow are free. We lost Absalom, but we got plenty of intel to sift through. The way I see it, we still came out ahead."

"This time, yes. But everything we know points to there being at least one leak in our ranks, maybe more."

"I think it would be safe to assume the Grays have multiple sources, probably operating without any awareness of each other. Different levels of access, different sources of information, so it's hard to pin down who is selling us out."

Dax nodded. "I agree, and so does Bahl. She did some very quiet digging and narrowed down the field a little for us."

"How narrow?"

Dax set down his comms on the desk and tapped in a command. A holographic display appeared in the air between them, filled with images of more than two dozen men and women. "This is everyone she could find who had access to the information about our mission to retrieve Nyx."

Kurt took a drink as he looked at the faces and names, the smooth flavor of the Scotch suddenly turning bitter as he realized he knew many of them.

Dax reached into the display and selected one of the images, making it expand. "She's at the top of the list. Remember her?"

Fraxx. It was Lieutenant Castille, the JAG officer who had sat in on Eric's interrogation. "I remember. Sharp mind, cool under pressure." *Soft hands. Nice curves. And a smile he hadn't been able to forget.*

"She was transferred here shortly before we went on that mission."

"She's JAG, though. Why would someone from the Judge Advocate Corps have access to that information?"

"That's a good question." Dax flicked to another image. It was a request for files. A lot of files. She'd been granted access to reports covering everything Team Three had done in the last twelve months, including their most recent missions.

He leaned in as he skimmed the document. "What the hell? Who authorized this?"

"The same man who sent her to represent Erben. Colonel Scott Archer."

Kurt rocked back in his chair. "Archer?"

Dax drained his glass before nodding. "Archer."

"Well. *Fraxx.*" He emptied his glass, too, then poured them both another. He'd been planning on asking Castille out for a drink once things had settled down. Not much chance of that happening now. Not until he was sure she wasn't working for the enemy, even though he didn't see her as the type. She'd been direct and open the one time they'd met. If she was targeting the team, he should have picked up something from her. That was his damned job.

"It gets better. Astek's new CEO is going to be hosting an event here next month. A big splashy three-day gala. She wants to get the remaining corporations all in one place to work out new deals and bury the proverbial hatchet. During that event, it will be announced that the IAF is expanding its presence here in the Drift. There's a new station being commissioned, and part of the fleet will be permanently stationed here to help stabilize the region."

"*Veth*. This place is going to be crawling with corporate bigwigs, IAF brass, and a small army of aides, assistants, and hangers-on. It's going to be a security nightmare."

"Which is why you're going to be attending as part of Archer's entourage."

"Please tell me you're joking."

"I'm not joking. I'm expected to send someone as a representative of Nova Force."

"Why aren't you sending Caldwell? Hobnobbing with snobs is encoded in his DNA." Crispen Charles Caldwell the 15th, was the oldest child of the current ruler of Cassien Alpha. Well, half of it, anyway.

"You're my XO and a highly decorated senior officer. Caldwell is only a lieutenant, and while he's better at small talk, he doesn't have your skill at reading people. This will put you in the perfect position to try and find our mole, or moles."

"And I can keep an eye on Archer while I'm at it." It was a good plan. He still hated it, though.

"Castille will be there, too. She's already been tapped as part of Archer's group."

Suddenly, this assignment didn't seem so bad. Three days with Castille might be enough time to work out whose side she was on, and what she was after. "Alright."

Dax cocked a brow. "Just like that? I figured I'd have to bribe you with extra time off."

"It needs to be done, and you're right, I'm the logical choice."

"Uh huh. And it has nothing to do with Lieutenant Castille's intriguing presence?"

"None."

Dax grinned. "You know, for an interrogator, you can't lie for shit. You should probably work on that."

"Lying takes too much effort. The truth is simpler."

"I hear you on that."

"Does this mission of mine have a name yet? Or is it off the record?" he asked a few minutes later.

"For now, it's off the record. We'll read in the others later." Dax raised his glass again. "But welcome to Operation Artemis."

They finished their drinks in companionable silence, both of them staring at the projected images of people they knew. At least one of them was working for the enemy. Dax had been right, they couldn't trust anyone outside their small circle, and that included a smart, sexy JAG officer by the name of Bobbi Castille.

***

Thank You for Reading OPERATION FURY!

I hope you enjoyed Eric and Nyx's story.
If you're looking for more stories like this one, I invite you to explore the other books in the Drift universe, which include both the Nova Force and Drift series.

ABOUT THE AUTHOR

Susan lives out on the Canadian west coast surrounded by open water, dear family, and good friends. She's jumped out of perfectly good airplanes on purpose and accidentally swum with sharks on the Great Barrier Reef.

If the world ends, she plans to survive as the spunky, comedic sidekick to the heroes of the new world, because she's too damned short and out of shape to make it on her own for long.

You can find out more about Susan and her books here:
www.susanhayes.ca